VARIETY
A Collection of Short Stories

VARIETY
A Collection of Short Stories

Dorothy Davies

VARIETY
A Collection of Short Stories

GRAVESTONE PRESS

TABLE OF CONTENTS

Winner Takes All

It started when Wayne (I've blanked out his somewhat rude nickname) Johnson walked into the Pig and Bucket at 7 o'clock on the last day of the month. What month doesn't matter, the fact it was the last day does.

It's been a tradition at the Pig and Bucket for as long as anyone could remember that whoever walked in at that time bought drinks for everyone there. Just the once, mind, one round of drinks.

It's been going on so long no one gave it a thought. Like, no one stood around and waited until 7 o'clock had gone, either. If they were out there and wanted a drink, they walked in and paid up. It was something we did.

The thing was… this night, the one when it all kicked off, someone walked in alongside Wayne. A stranger.

Everyone in the bar went silent like a switch had been turned off. Flick. Chatter stopped, glasses no longer clinked, feet did not shuffle on the sawdust.

Every head turned toward the door.

He was tall, the stranger; dark but not in the way you think, not like a dark man coming in but a man bringing in darkness. Oh, that sounds stupid but you know what I mean: if you've ever met someone that seems like they came from 'down there' rather than 'up there', you'll know just what I mean. I can't put it in proper words like those writer people can.

The doors on the Pig and Bucket open wide, so they do, it's possible for two people to walk in at the same time. The question – silently mouthed by every last drinker in the pub – was, which of them came in first? If it were the stranger, then we had a problem, 'cos trying to explain our weird tradition to them who don't know is pretty damn difficult.

Wayne turned to the dark man and said; "whoever walks in here at 7 on the last day of the month gets to buy everyone a drink, friend."

And the dark man said, "I am not your friend and you were a fraction ahead of me, sir."

Well now, I can't be remembering the last time anyone said 'sir' to Wayne, he being the biggest loser I know but still… it was polite, if nothing else. Wayne looked round for support but for once none of us had been watching the clock to see if anyone would come in at 7, so it was his word against the dark man. I wouldn't have put a bet on which one was right and I definitely wouldn't have argued with someone who looked like he came from somewhere not very nice, either.

But I'm not Wayne Johnson.

The talk started up again, low, almost self-conscious, drinks were being drunk and feet began to kick the sawdust into piles again. Everyone tried to act as if they weren't the least bit interested but they were; they all wanted that free drink off one or other of them. If the dark man played the game, of course.

"I walked in afore you." Wayne frowned at the stranger.

8

"Sir," he was nothing if not polite, "I walked in beside you. We entered the door at the same time. Now, should we not buy these gentlemen their drinks between us?"

"No."

The tone in Wayne's voice made the landlord, Chev, look up pretty darn quick, I can tell you. It meant *trouble* in the worst way. Wayne was an all right guy, even drunk he was an all right guy but get him on the wrong side no matter when and you had a handful of aggro any sane person would avoid.

The stranger wouldn't know that.

Chev leaned on the bar and looked at them both.

"Might I make a suggestion, you two?"

Wayne looked at him. "What?"

"Wayne, yo-" he stopped himself from using Wayne's nickname just in time. "Listen up. You two got a dispute here. Now either one of you leaves and the other one buys the drinks or you gamble for it. Toss a coin, perhaps?"

"Nah." Wayne dismissed both suggestions without even looking round at the stranger. I watched him, not Wayne and noticed his face didn't change.

"What would you suggest, sir?"

"Cards. Play you at cards. You do play, don'tcha?"

"I did."

"Then you can play again."

The other thing I noticed was everyone was nursing the last of their beers, not wanting a refill in case they had to pay for it. The chance of a free

9

drink was still on the table, as it were. If these two sorted out their differences.

Then I noticed something else, something I ain't told a living soul since that day. I saw *through* the stranger. For a second, he was like - a faded photograph. Then he was solid again and I thought, had too much strong beer, me. Not that it would stop me having another when this nonsense was sorted out.

"All right."

Wayne looked displeased for a moment, he ain't the world's greatest card player, he'd lose at Snap, for sure, but he suggested it and he had to go with it.

Chev put two beers on the counter, nodding at the two of them. "On the house, you can make up for it later, when you decide."

"Thanks." Wayne took his and drank half the glass down before he looked at the stranger. He hadn't even touched his. "You all right with the bet, sir?" and the 'sir' came out so sarcastic I would have given money to bet the stranger would land him one. He didn't. He inclined his head so slightly you hardly saw it.

"I am indeed." He picked up the beer and walked over to a small table away from everyone. The message was clear, keep out, this is private.

Wayne stomped over, banging his worn out boots on the floor as hard as he could as a way of showing disapproval. Tom Watkins, at the side of me as always, muttered "idiot. He could have paid up and looked big."

I had to agree with him.

Another silence fell over everyone like dust from the never cleaned rafters as the cards were shuffled and cut. Wayne drew the highest card, then they were dealt out.

Now you got to understand I didn't see the cards being laid out, I don't know who held which hand and who put what down. The game went on in near silence for a while, to the point when if drinks hadn't been at stake here, none of us would have sat around and waited patiently for it to end. We would have bought another drink and got on with our conversations, our 'setting the world to rights' talk which every true pub has on every true drinking night.

But we didn't and we watched and we saw from the body language that Wayne was not doing well. He was tense, holding himself very stiff, muttering under his breath, flicking non-existent dust off his jacket – like that would make a difference.

Then something was said and to this day no one knows what it was. What we do know is – Wayne pulled a knife and in a moment the dark stranger was on the floor, with his breath gone and his heart still. Like it was that quick. Before any of us could move, Wayne turned round and looked at us.

"What did I do?" he asked in such despair it near broke your heart.

Then someone shrieked or shouted or something and we all looked down. The stranger had gone.

And the knife Wayne held was black as sin and it never, from that day to this, showed a scrap of silver once.

Ghost? Revenant, someone said, lovely word, better than ghost any day. Revenant, but what was he doing in the Pig and Bucket and why did he take on Wayne's challenge?

Chev asked around and found out, about a month later, some dark seeming man had met a sorry end in the bar about a hundred years ago. Had he come back to live it out again? He was gone, we would never know.

We do know Wayne wasn't the same man ever again. In fact, he bought the drinks that night and we've hardly seen him since. The few times he does call in someone was bound sure to ask to see the knife, to see if it had gone back to being silver. It hadn't. It didn't.

I know. Wayne gave me the knife one afternoon, called round at my place, asked me to take it off him and keep it, only it was tormenting him, calling him to stab it right into his heart, like he stabbed the stranger and he knew if he kept it, he would.

I check it now and then.

That's how I know it's still black and I don't doubt for a minute it always will be.

The real big problem is, it's calling me now, faint but there. Like I should have stopped it. Like I had the chance to stop it.

Winner Takes All, they say. I think that time old Wayne won, in a manner of speaking, but then lost out big time. And giving the knife to me means

I lost out too. I guess I shouldn't have taken it but what do you do when a friend comes calling like that?

Got to admit to a bit of morbid curiosity, too. I wanted to see if it stayed black.

Black as the gleeful thought that went through my mind when the stranger was on the floor, dead as I thought, because he was a stranger. We don't overly care for them in the Pig and Bucket. Especially at 7 o'clock on the last day of the month.

Anyone know who I can pass the knife on to? Only the calling's getting a little louder these days.

Beauty Sleeps

It is the strangest thing that someone can be the love of your life, the one you cherish beyond all others, the one who holds your very soul in their fine delicate fingers that are like chains, so tight do they hold your priceless gift of love and yet you look at others.

It is so because I can do nothing else but go with the way nature made me.

Talk to me not of those who stay devoted to one person their entire married lives, talk to me not of those who fall in love, lose that loved one and never ever look at another person as long as they live.

I disbelieve them.

We are all born with the driving need to perpetuate the species. It is true, this I acknowledge, that men and women have used that excuse for eternity to justify their dalliances outside their relationships which were supposed to be everlasting. It is an excuse. It is also valid.

There are some who are driven by darker needs. Those of us who rise and fall with the waxing and waning of the moon phases, those of us who respond to the call of nature in different ways, those whose bodies change and whose resulting appearance is not entirely under their control. Ah, do you think, even now in this enlightened age, that such mythical creatures as werewolves, vampires, shape-shifters and the like are no more than myths? Do you not understand and accept that every myth, no matter how strange, has its basis in fact somewhere in the distant past, even if that past is as distant as the Stone Age and beyond?

Think on it now. Know that dragons once existed as dinosaurs did. Likewise unicorns and werewolves and all the other mythical creatures, mer-people, centaurs, need I go on?

You are asking about the other realms, fairies and the like. They have been with us since the world began; they are timeless, immortal and real. Ask no more. It is fact.

The facts are these.

For the first time in my existence I fell in love.

She was amazing, so beautiful the sun hid its face when she walked the earth.

So intelligent that philosophers stopped their philosophising and listened to her instead.

So joyful that the very birds stopped singing to let her celebrate life.

How trite are these descriptions, how cliché ridden! How truly awful! And yet there is no other way to describe the effect she had on the world – and on me. I was lost. Completely. For the first time I thought I had found someone who would truly hold my love and life for eternity.

In some ways I was right.

In other ways I was not.

We courted, we married, we lived. Within a year I was bored. Beauty at that level is boring as it has no imperfections. Perfection is hard to live with as you constantly measure yourself against it and find yourself lacking. I stared hard at the mirror some mornings and knew, handsome as I know I am, I could not match her perfection. When we had dinner parties or entertained in other ways, everyone looked at her and not at me.

The male ego is very easily damaged.

Her knowledge outshone mine. I could not hold an intelligent conversation with her; she would pin down my obvious faults and pour scorn on them.

I looked for others, less beautiful, less intelligent; less knowledgeable. I began to recover my equilibrium.

She suspected, of course.

I denied it, of course.

We continued in a state of truce for a further year when, to my horror, she announced the one thing I had not thought of – she was to have my child.

I should explain that I am not the kind of man who seeks perpetuity through a bloodline. I am not the kind of man who relishes the thought of his home being wrecked with baby items and his sleep wrecked through baby wailing and adoring fluttering people gushing over its every smile, burp and frown.

I took care of that. Knowledge she might have, sense when it comes to the male ego she does not. I took care that she did not discover what had been fed to her and mourned with her at the loss of the child.

But possibly not good enough, for soon after I realised her eyes had turned to another. For a while I encouraged it, the pressure being taken from me,

16

which suited me well but then it galled me that she would look elsewhere.

It was time to take the next step.

The person who supplied the material to induce the miscarriage supplied further material for me.

It worked.

I had her buried, so we had a grave to mourn over and cherish; those of us who professed to love her. I had her buried because I liked the idea of beauty asleep in a grave.

I imagined her rotting, slowly, everything eating her away, slowly.

I played the field after a due period of mourning had passed. I had fun, something I had forgotten about and could do.

But something was troubling me. Something I felt I had overlooked. Something I should have known – but didn't.

A friend commented that I knew, of course, she was not dead, but sleeping. This was a religious comment and I ignored it. At first. He persisted, telling me over and over that she was not dead but sleeping.

The word 'vampire' was mentioned.

I laughed.

Then I recalled the time I cut myself and she fastened onto the cut and sucked it until I thought she would take the finger clean off my hand.

I wondered why I had been foolish enough not to recognise my own kind.

I had to do something. My mind would not rest.

One dark overcast storm tossed night I took shovel and courage and went to her grave. I dug and dug until I uncovered the coffin, untouched, unscarred by its internment.

I prised off the coffin lid and looked down at her perfect face. She looked up at me - and smiled.

Shiloh

His father's fist exploded into his face. Jonathan fell against the stone wall, feeling blood and tears spurt simultaneously. Pain flared and blinded him. Through the haze he heard the angry voice beating at his ears, at his mind.

"I said, get out and milk the sheep! I care not if it's Garrett's turn! In this house what I say is done!"

Jonathan heard his brother snigger, heard a page turn in the precious book, the one he so longed to look at, to learn to read. The pain was such that he dared not speak, dared not risk more blows. He pressed a hand to his face, struggled to his feet and made his way through the opening into a biting wind.

For a moment the cold bit into the pain and intensified it, then it began to numb so he could look around, could breathe slightly easier. Jonathan thrust a hand into his tunic and brought it out empty. No rag. The blood would have to flow. He dashed away shameful tears with the back of his hand. Cold. Bitter, bitter cold. Now, if he were Donald he could turn into the wind, tell which direction it was from and guess how long it would last. But he wasn't Donald and it made little difference anyway. Cold, not cold, he still had to milk a few ewes to provide something for the evening meal or risk more punishment at his father's hands.

Jonathan kicked angrily at a stone in his path. It wasn't so much the blows, but Garrett's sniggering that hurt. Just because he had been chosen for *learning* while Jonathan was left to *labour*, was that any reason to laugh? But then that was Garrett's way his creeping please-everyone way of getting through life. Perhaps I should try it; perhaps I could avoid some problems if I did. He shook his head, forgetting for a moment the hurt that would cause.

Fool! He inwardly raged. Fool to be hurt, fool to do things to make the hurt worse. Fool to be out here, cold, lonely, when there could have been a chance at *learning,* if I hadn't thrown it all away with idling.

Rooks cawed raucously overhead, circling madly, swirling, dipping; flying upward in a thick cloud. Would that I were a rook, thought Jonathan sadly, would that I could fly away from pain and cold and hunger. And from being no one but Jonathan, fit for punching, fit for nothing but milking a ewe now and then. Would that I could fly away from stupid, thick-headed, hateful sheep.

The flock had scattered itself all over the plain. The vegetation was sparse, even sheep had to work hard at finding enough to eat. Jonathan stared at them, hating them yet envying their thick wool coats. No matter how much he put on, he always seemed to feel cold.

Someone waved to him from the lea of the sheep pen and he hurried toward the only shelter around.

"Come and sit with me!" Estel said, her small, pinched face looking as cold as he felt. As Jonathan

20

slumped down beside her, she took one of his cold hands in hers and began to rub. "Oh your poor face!"

"Father didn't like me saying it was Garrett's turn to come out."

"Perhaps it would be better not to argue with him, Jonathan."

His nose and cheek bone began to ache with a vicious blinding pain that filled his head.

"If I say nothing, he hits me for not standing up for myself. So I answer back. It's better than giving in."

"Did you come to milk the ewes?" There was a hint of laughter in Estel's voice that Jonathan recognised instantly. Mocking again. Despite her apparent kindness, Estel always mocked him, making him feel useless, small, childish.

"I did." He looked at his empty hands. "And without a pail, too."

"Anyone would, with a face like yours at the moment. It's a wonder you remembered the way to the sheep! Borrow mine. We can always swap back later. I'll stop by your place and borrow yours in a while."

"And tell him I forgot?"

The answering smile was soft, understanding.

"I'll think of something, never fear."

The stones at his back were hard, jagged, the ground unforgiving and cold, but Jonathan felt at ease for the first time in the long, lonely day. Estel understood; she was older than him and wiser in so many things. It was good to have someone who understood, someone who spoke kindly to him, someone who remembered he was a human being and not an automaton working endlessly and seemingly for nothing at all. For all the work, was not the Tribe still cold, hungry and declining fast?

From his place by the sheep pen, Jonathan could not see the borders of the plain. It was an endless flat landscape which had no boundaries, no definitions; no limits that his mind could fasten onto. He felt overawed by it.

"What is this place?" he asked suddenly, startling Estel who had fallen into some kind of doze.

"What place, Jonathan?"

"This." He waved toward the open plain, the vast sky.

"This place where we live? It's called Shiloh, it's an old, old place where once a battle was fought between tribes, so the Elder said."

Her words brought a sudden bitterness to Jonathan, an acid taste to his mouth.

"See? You know so much more than I do; I know nothing. I never will know anything!"

"Jonathan, it's the way of the Tribe that some shall learn and some shall labour. You know that. Perhaps when you're a man…"

"Then it will be too late! Then there will be work all the time, just like now, but there will be a mate to care for as well. Why did I throw away my chance?"

"Would that we knew the answers to all these questions." Estel laughed softly. "Look, Jonathan, I give you a little secret of mine. I was not chosen for *learning* but I hurried my work, I lingered on the

22

edge of lessons, I stood at the door of the Teaching House and I learned."

"I wonder if I could-" Jonathan fell back against the wall, the ache overwhelming everything, all thought, all feeling. "No, I'm useless. Look at me, didn't think to bring a pail for the milking."

"It takes some growing, this thing called thinking," she said and Jonathan knew she mocked him again.

That evening, when most were tucked away in their homes, sitting round fires carefully fed with dried grass and dung, Jonathan sat outside his home, staring up at the bitter brightness of the night sky, turning over Estel's words. There could be time, he could make time, perhaps – He suddenly stood up and tugged his fur cloak tight around his body. I know where I can go, I know who to talk to.

Grandmother sat as close to the fire as she dared, feeding the flames delicately, tiny pieces of wood held in her wrinkled old fingers.

"Ah, tis Jonathan. Not often you come to see me, boy."

"I know, Grandmother, and it's not for the fact of not wanting to."

"I know, boy, I know. If there isn't work to do, then you're tired out from all the work you have to do. Too much work for you youngsters. And I lived in hope the work would get easier, the living better."

"I don't mind the work, Grandmother, it's just that-" He sank down on the plaited rush mat and poured out his loneliness and longing.

23

"I can't think of simple things, like taking a pail to milking. I can't remember things, like weather prediction. I want to learn, but I gave away my chance of learning. I want to be someone, I want to be clever, I want to be-"

She rested her hand on his head for a moment and he felt as if he drew comfort and strength from her touch.

"Everyone has something special to do in this life, Jonathan. Sometimes it takes a long time for the finding out, but it is always there. Look at me, an old woman, fit for no man, but you come for advice and others come for advice, too. So there is my place in this Tribe. Yours, well, yours perhaps is still to come."

"I can't wait, Grandmother."

"Ah but you can, boy. You can. We all have to wait."

"What are *you* waiting for?" The words came out sharper than he intended, but his grandmother didn't seem to mind.

"Why, Jonathan, at my age, I'm waiting to die."

He was humbled and silenced by her words.

During the next few days Jonathan thought of Estel's words and began to hurry his work. There was one day when work took up all his time from rising to sleeping, but there were times, minutes strung like catkins on a branch, when he could creep close to the Teaching House and listen to some words from the Elder.

After a few days, he realised it was not the teaching he came for, but an object he had not noticed in his early youth. He came to stare at the thing hanging from the ceiling. A large round thing, a circle covered with something that looked like skin, might have been skin, and yet –

All Jonathan knew was his whole body, his entire being, longed with an intensity that hurt to touch the object, to handle it, to – to own it?

He ran fast, pounding his feet into the rough flinty soil, deliberately sending shock waves through his body and into his head, anything to dull the terrible, terrible thought that had entered his mind – and stayed there.

He stopped, breathless, almost doubled up with the agony in his side, chilled despite the running and still the thought remained. In the loneliness of the wind-swept plain, he gave voice to the thought.

"Whatever it is, I want it. I feel it is rightly mine," but he knew he could tell no one – no one at all – of his thought of his dream.

Still he could not stay away, could not leave that object hanging there. He came to stare, to silently worship it. But people began to notice, to talk.

"What's this about wasting time?" His father stood tall over him, the dull brutish mouth working in anger.

"I don't waste time. I do my work."

Surprisingly, his mother came to his defence, the first time he could ever remember her doing such a thing.

"Leave the boy be, I hear no talk of his wasting time." She turned away, taking no further part in the confrontation. But her words, her unexpected intervention, deflated the man's anger and he turned and stomped to his fireside.

"All right, but let this be an end of it, standing staring in the Teaching House like one without his wits."

Garrett laughed and crept closer to his father.

"He would like to be one of the *learning* ones, Father."

"Ha, fine chance he has of that!"

Jonathan shot his brother a venomous look. Nasty little person, always creeping around the adults, anything to curry favour. He stalked out of the house, went looking for his grandmother.

"What is that thing which hangs in the Teaching House?" he asked as he sipped scalding tea.

"You've been looking. I've heard the talk. That's a drum, boy."

"What's it for?"

"What's it for? Gracious, how would anyone know such a thing? 'Tis just something left over from *Before*. No one knows what it's for and no one's allowed to touch it, either."

Her warning held dire consequences for anyone foolish enough to ignore it.

Soon there was new talk to divert Jonathan's mind from the drum. It permeated every part of life; from grunted conversations over scanty meals to words he caught standing on the edge of lessons or out in the wild with the flock. There was trouble pending with the Hill Tribe. The talk was not of peace but of fighting, defending the plain.

26

How can we defend this? Jonathan stared at the endless rolling land going on to the very edge of the known world. There's enough for all of us, isn't there?

"No." Grandmother was emphatic, sitting with hands wrapped tight around a steaming cup, trying to drag its warmth into her ageing body. "It isn't enough. The land is poor, vegetation isn't good, 'tis just enough for our sheep and our food. We let the Hill people in, there'll be nothing left. Besides," she added, almost spitting the words into the night, "they aren't fit to be associated with." She would say no more on the subject, despite Jonathan's questions.

"No," said the Elders at the next *Gathering*. "There can be no talk of peace with people like that. Why should we talk peace? It is they who are threatening to invade the plain. Let them stay where they are, in the hills where they belong."

"But the food has run out," objected the sullen representative the Hill Tribe had sent to the *Gathering*. "There's no pasture left for our animals. We starve."

"And if you come onto the plain, we starve too," snapped an Elder. "You made your choice, now live with it!"

The Hill Tribe man left, muttering curses that sent shudders down Jonathan's spine. The Hill people were tough, hardy and said to be expert fighters. What chance did quiet peaceful Plains people have to defend themselves?

In moments of fantasy, out among the sheep, Jonathan imagined himself marching at the head of a large crowd, leading them to battle and to victory. "Jonathan!" they cried in loud, triumphant voices. "Jonathan, our saviour, our leader!" But it was not loud, triumphant voices Jonathan heard, it was the lonely keening cry of a kestrel riding the clouds, seeking its food, safely away from all who would prey on it.

As we ought to be, thought Jonathan. But no, that thought didn't fit well in his mind. Back came the picture of the crowd, with Jonathan at its head. The picture fitted well but there was something missing, some – thing – some – sound missing. Try as he might the missing piece would not fall into place.

Came a morning of bright bitter sunshine, cold as if from the very jaws of Hell itself. Came a morning of preparation, when every man looked to whatever weapons he had, a club, a stone, a sharp honed flint. Came a moment when the men gathered themselves into a crowd and began to move, limp of foot, unsure of mind, exuding fear.

Jonathan stood, shaking from head to foot, full of confidence, as sure as if he had heard the words from the Great Deity Himself. He ran to the Teaching House and snatched down the drum. No one stopped him, no one cried out in protest at what he did. There was a rightness about it that could not be said, nor stopped.

With this we can beat the Hill people, he thought, running to catch up with the men. With this we can beat them, but I must be there.

28

He gained on the crowd of men, he passed them; he marched at the head.

The Plains people moved out across hard bitten ground, lifting their feet, swinging their arms, sure of victory, sure of strength, marching to the steady pounding beat of the proud drummer boy of Shiloh.

This story is dedicated with respect and admiration to the greatest SF and Fantasy writer of all time, Ray Bradbury, who planted this particular seed many years ago with his story
"The Little Drummer Boy of Shiloh."

All Down The Lonely Years

Charles Grey walked slowly toward the school, arms swinging loosely in the disjointed shambling walk the old sometimes assume. The sun silvered the thick tight curls clustered around the bald patch, a halo of unconventional colour. The pavements were hot; his old shoes were no protection against bubbling tar. Already his tie felt as if it were confining his throat and pulling the collar into his neck.

He was almost there. Soon he would turn the corner by the old Oxfam shop, blank-faced and dusty and then he would be able to see the stone wall surrounding the playground, topped with multi-coloured heads calling greetings to those approaching, yelling goodbyes to those departing. Same every day. Didn't they ever tire of it?

"Hello, Mr. Grey!" Children ran to his side, catching hold of his hands, spilling talk and laughter as easily as the sun slid through the branches of the sturdy oak shading one playground corner. He listened to the excited talk until he reached the door, then he paused for a moment to allow the children to drop back and let him enter the coolness of the corridor. He blinked in the shade suddenly imposed on his old eyes and found his way to the classroom by instinct.

The heat was stifling. He opened the windows and the door leading to the courtyard at the back, to let some of the slight hot breeze move through the chalk and schoolbook dusty room. He rearranged the papers on his desk, looking up only when he heard the bell, calling the children into pushing jostling lines ready to file into class.

And morning lessons began.

In the staff room at break time he drank tea, listened to teacher gossip complaining about classes or muttering about the Head's new rules, but he wasn't really listening, just letting the talk drift over his head. It was so hot he almost wished it was his turn for playground duty so he could walk outside. But that would have meant treading the hot asphalt and children holding on with sweaty hands. Perhaps it was better to stand at the window and feel the breeze touching his face.

Lunchtime was the rest period. He would leave the school and walk narrow country lanes, staring out across deserted fields, burning and cracking open in the heat. His bald patch turned red under the sun's rays and he wished he had some kind of hat. An hour was just long enough to stroll, to pick a long grass to chew, to listen to the birds and insects, before making his way back for his favourite afternoon session, English, and story time to finish the day. It was everything he wanted out of life. He would let the rich language roll from his tongue and even if it did go over the heads of some of the children, they savoured the sound and feel of the writers –

"Who knew their craft, by God!" he would announce in the staff room, knowing even as he did so that he was adding another layer to his reputation as an old fogey. It didn't matter. The children loved it and so did he. The school could go take a running jump at itself if it thought he would give up his story time for anyone!

When the reluctant hands of the clock finally touched 3.15, the children poured, shouting, into the playground to find their waiting mothers. The school would sigh with relief as the last pounding feet left the corridors to settle in dust and silence for the night.

Charles Grey walked alone round the school, touching dust-covered desks, disturbing a pile of books precariously balanced these long, lonely years and a single tear escaped to run unheeded down his face. How long had he been coming here, day after day, acting out the ritual of teaching a class full of children who longer came, children who now sat at home before the all-powerful, infallible screen?

Damn the things to hell! he thought savagely.

"Hey Mister, what're you doing here?"

The black hair flopped down over the button bright eyes of the boy who stared at him. Charles stared back. He had heard no sound; the boy had appeared as if by magic.

"I could ask – what are *you* doing here?"

"My telescreen's broke; I came out for something to do."

"I'm remembering what it was like to teach here."

The boy perched on the edge of a desk, tipping the legs off the ground. Charles closed his throat on the sharp words before they left his mouth. It wasn't his school any longer; he had no more right to be here than the boy.

"What's that?" asked the boy, after very carefully scrutinising Charles.

"What's what?"

"Teach – whatever you said."

"Your telescreen shows you how to do things, doesn't it? How to write, draw, add up?"

"That's right."

"I used to do all that here, with a lot of children."

"Does that mean you know as much as the telescreen?"

Charles laughed. "Well, not as much as your telescreen, perhaps, but I knew enough to teach the children."

"My name's Terry." In a sudden burst of friendliness and trust the boy thrust out a grubby hand and Charles took it without a flicker of hesitation.

"I'm Charles."

The bond of friendship was sealed in that moment. Charles looked into the open face; the smile spangled with freckles and felt his heart turn over. This would make pretence even harder, knowing there were still bright-eyed boys around who were curious enough to come looking in the old school.

"What was it like?" asked Terry, looking around at the inches-thick dust encrusted on everything. "And why is that desk the only clean one?"

Charles smiled, a little self-consciously. "Play-acting at my age needs props. I use the desk when I'm pretending to teach."

"Were all these desks for the children?" Terry counted them, his eyes wide with astonishment. "Twenty-five? Were there twenty-five children – in this one room?"

"Yes."

"Golly gosh! I've never seen twenty-five children together anywhere, except on the telescreen. Wasn't it noisy?"

"Sometimes, but not when they were all reading or writing or listening to my story."

The boy glanced down at the watch swinging from his belt. Then he jumped up, letting the desk crash back to the floor. It raised puffs of dust.

"Hey, time's getting on. I'd better be going. They'll be worrying about me. Look, will you be here tomorrow afternoon?"

"Yes, I'll be here tomorrow afternoon."

With that promise in his ears, Terry was gone, feet banging through the dusty corridors, swing doors slamming after him. Charles caught a glimpse of the black head bobbing along the other side of the wall, then all was quiet again.

"A boy!" Charles told the silent, dusty room. "A real live boy who never once said I was a silly old fool for playing out a fantasy. It feels like a dream!" But his heart was lighter as he carefully locked the school doors and set off for home, the promise of tomorrow in his eyes.

For three days Terry came in the afternoons, banging through the old swing doors, shouting his greeting along dusty corridors that echoed his voice. Together the old man and boy bridged the gap of years, poring over dusty browning books, rustling pages in the afternoon heat of the lovely summer days. Terry laughed at words that stayed still, watched with amusement as Charles chalked simple mathematics on the blackboard and wiping them off with the eraser as cleanly as the processor cleared the screen for another lesson. For three days Charles felt as if the clock had been turned back; he was a complete person again, doing what he had always loved best.

At the end of the third afternoon, Terry scuffed his feet and looked out of the window, hesitating.

"My telescreen's been fixed; I start lessons again tomorrow."

"That's all right, Terry." The lump in his throat threatened to choke him. He turned away, pretending that the mist in front of his eyes was the heat haze.

"I've – I've really enjoyed the lessons." Terry seemed afraid of the emotion he could feel from Charles, as if not sure how to handle it.

"Thank you. It's been good to teach again for a while."

"Will you still come here?"

"I expect so." Charles took a deep breath and turned back to look at the trusting, sad face. "I've been doing it for a long time. No one seems to care and it gives me something to do."

35

"It must be lonely, being old." And for a moment seemed as if the sadness was almost too much for Terry to bear.

"It is." Charles forced a smile which didn't reach his eyes. "Thank you, Terry; you gave me back my past for a little while. Go on with you now. Your family will start worrying about you again. I'll be all right. I'll be here when the telescreen breaks down again."

"Sure." Terry got up, anxious not to delay the parting, seeming to want to be alone. "Bye, Charles." And for the last time Terry ran from the classroom, pounding the dusty corridors, letting the doors swing shut behind him.

It was a long time before Charles could bring himself to leave the empty room, still filled with Terry's vibrant energy and youth. Tomorrow would be emptier than ever before. At last he slowly locked the doors and windows and left with a heavy tread.

The next day Charles stood at the window, not even attempting to pretend he was there for any other reason than to grieve for the friendship he had found – and so quickly lost.

"I shouldn't have come," he told himself. "The dream's gone, everything's changed. I'll never be able to imagine it again."

Suddenly he thought he heard Terry calling and shook his head. He was dreaming; he had to be. Terry was at home, studying in front of the faceless soulless telescreen.

"Come on, Gran, he's in here! He said he'd be here." Terry burst through the door, radiating excitement. Behind him came an old lady, hair as white as his own, face wreathed in wrinkles and smiles.

"Charles, this is my Gran. She's lonely too."

A touching of hands, a mutual smile. Charles felt his depression slip away. Perhaps the long years wouldn't be so lonely after all…

This story is dedicated, with respect and admiration, to the memory of the great SF writer Isaac Asimov, who planted a seed many years ago with his story "The Fun They Had" published in an edition of F&SF. In the story children had a telescreen to give them their lessons and, having discovered 'real' books and schools were sad to think of the fun those children had had and the lonely lives the modern children led. I took that theme and created my own version as a tribute to another great writer.

In the Beginning

'In the beginning was the mushroom cloud, many trees' tall into the sky and from the cloud came fine dust. It burned the ground and tore the skin from the bones of those who ran.'

IT stood in the centre of the square in its own hut, the wooden casing marked with rain, the flimsy back which housed the electronics slowly dissolving, colourful wires falling out.

'There were some people who ran to burrow in the ground like the rabbit in his hole, there to live until the dust should cease to fall.'

Gil hated IT. He didn't know why and he didn't feel he could tell anyone how he felt, either. It was just a blind hatred for a blind thing. The blank stare disconcerted him and he would make elaborate detours to reach his hut rather than pass IT by.

"There were some people who fell to their knees and cried to the Unseen Spirit. It heeded not their cries and they were burned. Their bones littered the ground.'

Mother would complain if yet again he was late with the precious copper bowl full of water, but somehow it seemed, well, childish, to tell her that he didn't want to walk past IT. She would laugh at him and at thirteen it hurt to be laughed at, even by his mother. Or was it because she was his mother? But detour he would. And he did.

"There were some people who ran to the woods, where they lived as the animals do, sleeping on the ground and eating of the berries and leaves of the trees and bushes. Of these, many died, but some lived. They that lived joined with others who came from their holes in the ground. There was a Gathering together of those that did not die.'

"Where have you been? Why are you always so late with the water?" Annoyed, his mother went back into the shadowy interior of the hut, still grumbling about her need to tend to Zita and how late he was. Gil sat on the ground outside, picking at the grass.

"Look after Zita for me while I milk the cow." Before he could reply, she walked away, stoop-shouldered and tired, down the narrow beaten track toward the pasture. Were all the women stoop-shouldered and tired? He knew the answer even as he framed the question. Gil was growing up fast and questioning every aspect of his life. He was worried by the things he thought about.

'When the people ran to hide, they took nothing with them but their skills and when the dust was gone and there was silence in the world, they went back to look in the broken buildings for that which was of value. They found many things.'

Where in this Gathering is there a suitable mate for me? Gil asked himself. The girls were young and thin, not one of them seemed ready to help build a hut and start a new corner of this Gathering. If there should be no suitable mate… He examined the thought of leaving: it filled him with dread.

'There were books, many books, which told of the ways to build the things which made the mushroom cloud. In their anger and hate they burned all the books. They made fires which could be seen for many trees' distance. More people came to bring books to the Burning. It went on for many days.'

Zita gurgled and chuckled to herself and Gil went to pick her up. For a baby sister she wasn't so bad, at least she wasn't missing any vital parts and she might one day be as pretty as her name. He waved a flower in front of her eyes to amuse her and she reached out to grab it from him.

'And they found the Television, which we were once proud to care for in our Gathering. It was one of the earliest founder members who discovered it, complete among many broken ones. May his name live forever.'

His mother came back, walking slowly so as not to spill a single drop of the precious milk. That would be for Zita, it always was. Gil's young stomach rumbled with the need for the food he had

40

not had for the past two days. The harvest had been bad this season and the pasture was getting scarce.

"Everything's all right," he said as his mother passed him. "I was just playing with her. She didn't cry."

"There's a funeral this afternoon," his mother commented as she disappeared into the hut with Zita.

Gil followed her in. "Anyone I know?"

"An old man. I don't think you ever spoke to him."

Gil sighed wearily. A funeral meant a compounding of the nightmare which tormented his sleep. In the dream the black stare of IT came closer and closer, threatening to engulf him. The dead person's face would be captured in the square box and Gil would rise up from his bed, screaming. For, after every funeral, IT was brought out into the open, available for any bereaved grieving person to commune with it.

They say that in the time before the cloud came down, all the persons in the world had a Television. They say that people walked and talked behind the screen. They say the picture came from far away, people would talk to the screen and it would answer them. It must have been a wonderful thing.'

In the afternoon the male members of the Gathering – Gil among them – took their sharp pointed sticks and tramped into the forest to the burying ground. There they scraped the hard earth away to make a shallow grave. The Leader of the

Gathering came with the men who carried the body and they slowly lowered it into the cold unyielding earth.

Every member of the Gathering came forward, took a handful of earth from the side of the grave and threw it on the body. Then they turned and walked away.

The burying was silent, sombre. Gil knew that the nightmare would return that night, whether he had known the old man or not.

'The Television stood in the centre of the Place we had then and all who passed IT revered it. The hut was sheltered. IT was never left to fall apart. The children were taught to stay away from IT. IT stood proudly among us and we were proud that it was there.'

Gil ran with his friend Dani, tossing a ball from one to the other, then, thrusting it inside a rough home-made tunic to climb trees, Gil joined Dani and they swung dangerously from creaking branches before dropping to the hard earth where they could watch the blazing sun die in the vermillion sky.

"At the end of the day comes the dying," Gil sang softly.

Dani laughed. "Been listening to the Song Man too much!"

"I like the Song Man," Gil defended himself vigorously. "I like the Story Man, too."

"He only talks of the past," said Dani with all the confidence of fourteen years. "I look forward, not back."

"Don't we all?" responded Gil, showing – outwardly at least – equal confidence.

"Gil…" Dani rolled on his back and stared at the black lace pattern of branches on burning sky. "I want to talk to you…"

"You're talking; I'm listening, what's new?"

"No, serious talk now. You won't tell anyone, will you?"

"I won't tell."

Dani stared at Gil. His eyes were serious behind the curtain of red hair as he sought for a way to begin.

"Do you like Zita?"

"Zita? Well, of course I do, she's my sister, isn't she?"

"Han's my brother but I hate him." Dani dropped the startling statement into the late afternoon and both boys were silent. Gil turned the words over his mind.

"I don't hate Zita, she's just there, like Pati or Toni or Geri or any of the rest of them."

"I don't hate my family, Gil, Only Han. That twisted body, that - that blank stare, he's not right, Gil, I think he should have been left out for the dogs only Mother's too soft. She fusses over him; he gets all the milk while the rest of us go hungry! He's useless; he'll never be any good for the Gathering."

For a long moment Gil wondered how to respond to his friend's confession. Finally, words rose unbidden before he could stop them.

"I hate IT, Dani. I hate IT for its blank stare and strange shape but I can't say anything. IT doesn't get milk but it does get a lot of attention and songs and stories. I think we should get rid of it."

"Both of us with a hate and nothing we can do about it..."

"There is, if we had nerve enough to do it!" Gil became animated as a series of pictures crossed his mind. "You could leave Han on the edge of the woods, go for a pee or something, you can't be blamed for that, can you? And I could... smash... IT..."

White-faced, Dani stared at him. "You're talking about killing, Gil," he said softly, seriously.

"I know what I'm talking about but we're only talking, aren't we?

"Sure we are, sure we are, Gil. Come on, let's go home. It's getting late."

There were those in the Gathering who communed with the Television, who saw in the face many visions of the future. These people became Vision Men and spoke among us of that which is to come. There were many who fell down before the Television and worshipped it as being the silent voice of the Unseen Spirit."

On the day of Han's funeral, Gil walked with Dani, one arm round his shoulders, trying to comfort him. The Gathering mourned the loss of the man-child and brought loss-gifts to Dani's parents as they sat weeping in front of their hut.

44

Dani hid in the darkness, nursing his wild thoughts and guilt and Gil left him alone.

There was nothing he could say now; perhaps later, when the wound began to heal. Gil walked alone in the forest, listening to the howling dogs. Nursing his own hatred, he wondered if he had the nerve to carry out his own killing.

That night, when the nightmare came, the tiny face captured in the television screen was Han's blank-eyed stare. Gil sat up, struggling to control his scream and he knew what he had to do. Cautiously he crept from the coverings and made his way to the door, picking up his pointed stick as he went. No-one moved. There was only the soft breathing and murmuring of sleep in the darkness. Gil turned away, ignoring the inner voice that pleaded with him to stay and set out for the centre of the Place.

Han's family had gone; there was nobody to commune with IT. The filtered moonlight turned the glass face to silver. IT seemed to glare at Gil, as if IT knew what he had come for; almost sentient, a travesty of life...

Gil stood; stick poised, thinking about the nightmare, the devotion and care lavished on IT, a useless, inanimate object, unnecessary, backward-looking. The hate boiled over and he plunged the stick into the silver face. There was a sound like breaking ice on a winter's morning and, with ringing shouts of triumph, he smashed at IT again and again, splintering the wooden case, spilling the mysterious things inside down onto the ground.

As he stood staring at the wreckage he suddenly became aware of eyes on him. He spun round.

The Gathering had been woken by his shouts and the noise of the breaking machine and now they ringed the centre of the Place; silent, reproachful, accusing, hate-filled faces...

"Look!" Gil cried, his boy's voice edged with maturity. "I've destroyed IT, you're free!" The hostility grew, a tangible thing reaching out for him and he backed away, treading on things that snapped under his weight. He pleaded with the silence for understanding.

"You don't have to worry about IT, you don't have to tell the children to stay away from IT —oh don't you understand, you're free!"

No one answered him.

Clutching his stick tightly, he stood; television debris all around him, watching the Gathering fade back into the darkness and letting the night-breeze dry his tears.

'*There was one among us who did not understand or revere the Television. It is said by some he was disturbed by the death of a man-child in the Gathering, but yet others say the night winds took his mind. Yet others again say he could not comprehend the true meaning of the Television or of the Unseen Spirit that spoke from IT. The reasons are many, the facts are few. In the dark of a night when the winds are abroad to steal a man's mind from his body and leave it vacant, he went forth with his stick and attacked the Television.*

And it died.'

Loneliness Is A Personal Thing

"I think it's Monday 27th September. I wonder why I'm bothering to keep any kind of calendar and why I persist in recording a diary. Perhaps it's part of a subconscious plan to keep me sane. Who knows? Does it matter? After I recorded my diary last night, I took Jerry for a walk along the beach. It was pretty cold. The nights are getting colder already."

The waves were begging hands, outflung along the sand, touching, beseeching, getting nothing, withdrawing into the greenness that I remember once as being blue grey water. Perhaps one day I'll find out why it went green. Perhaps.

"Jerry loves the sea. He leaps about in the waves, biting the white tops, barking at the big breakers that threatened to crush him with their sheer size, running free before they break."

Jerry helps keep me sane, too.

"Got a load of dog food in today, went over to the industrial estate north of here, plenty of stores there. Just have to work out where to keep it."

Upstairs? Third bedroom might do, if I organise it properly. Cartons stack, don't they? Need all the tinned food I can find, along with calor gas, batteries, paraffin, logs, tablets for purifying the water, warm clothes. That's some shifting, girl... at least I won't put any weight!

"Spent my usual hour dialling telephone numbers. Did 10 pages today, I'm up to TR already."

Stupid daily penance. Stupid to hope that one day someone will answer me. Probably won't be able to do it for much longer anyway, as it is, it's a miracle that any of the exchanges are still working.

"Jerry scared off a pack of dogs today. Hope they leave us alone. I don't want to start shooting them."

Soft eyed Labradors, perky eared terriers, sad mongrels, ragged Afghan hounds, little ones, big ones, oh if only I could open loads of tins of food and make friends with them all! But, like the cats, they've all gone wild.

"Brought home some new CDs -- Dire Straits, Genesis, Gerry Rafferty, Elvis Presley, good additions to the collection. Come winter I'll have music and books, heat and light, food and clothes. Not like last winter."

Not like last winter. Poor Jerry, trusting puppy, cold and hungry, pushing against my legs, me clinging to him in the dark, listening to the gale -- never again! It's been a long summer, but we've made, Jerry and I, a lot of hard work, a lot of driving, but we'll be okay this time.

"Sometimes I wonder what I'd do if someone did answer their phone. Would I say' Hey, come on over, the house is plenty big enough, I've fitted it up with everything I need.' Or would I say, 'nice talking to you, glad to know that someone else is alive," and put the phone down? Do I want anyone else here now? What would Jerry do if someone else came too? I think he'd be jealous."

If a man answered, would the woman in me cry out for the strength of his body, possibly his love?

49

If a woman answered, would the lonely me cry out for her gossip and chat, possibly a friendship?

Yes... no.

No... yes.

It hasn't happened yet and I don't think it will. I'll decide when it does. The day the ringing stops and someone says? Hello?' I don't like being alone.

Who's going to listen to my tapes in years to come? Look at the row I've made already. Perhaps when I'm old, I'll sit and listen to my young voice and wonder whether the years went. Or will I cut my foot off with the axe, drive over the cliff in a gale, be eaten by a pack of starving dogs, become fatally ill with something the books can't tell me how to cure? What would Jerry do if I die? Go wild like the other dogs? What will I do when Jerry dies ... Get another pup and tame it, of course.

Of course.

"Train of thought, thinking of me, old, listening to these tapes of me, young. Will the woman who listens to these tapes in years to come understand why this woman, now aged 38 and lonely, still washes her hair every other day, uses make-up, wears exquisite jewellery and beautiful clothes? Will she understand why I couldn't leave the jewellery sitting on velvet pads, looking disdainfully at the world, but took it for myself, boxes of shining silver and imperial gold."

Will; the woman who listens to these tapes remember the ache of unshed tears, the burning, dry eyed lump I seem to carry always; will she recall how the arms ached for a child?

"Continuing train of thought, 'old' reminds me of the fact there was a skeleton over near the warehouse, the first I've seen for a long time. I would have thought that by now the wind and the dogs would have dispersed any that were left. I wonder how long it's been there, could it be someone I missed in my telephoning sessions?"

Foolish question to ask a tape! When did I start phoning? Earlier this year, wasn't it? The tapes would tell me, if I wanted to listen to them again. I'm sure it was earlier this year, after that black and terrible morning, when the clouds hung over the land as heavy as they hand over my mind. I remember...

Reaching for the pills, they were so close, then Jerry knocked the phone over. I thought, don't do that, someone might ring!

Do you know, Jerry, I spent all morning ringing numbers? Started at A, didn't I, and fool that I am, I've been doing it every day since, haven't I? I know, your eyes are telling me that you think your mistress is as foolish as I think she is, too.

Now the pills are here, around my neck, in case the axe, the car or the dogs get me.

So I blame you for my lonely life, Jerry! Big pink tongue lolls out, eyes watch my every move, a paw rests on my foot. My shadow, my doppelgänger, my lifeline to sanity. I wonder if I really meant to do it or was it a false alarm, even for me? Another foolish question.

"I went to church today for the first time since I found myself alone... it was thick with dust, dead flowers powdering away in vases, hymn and prayer

51

books mouldering in the pews. I lit the candles on the altar and knelt at the communion rail. A draught or something flickered the flames and there were ghosts. But I didn't pray."

Oh yes, there were ghosts all right, did I not feel Jerry's hackles rise as he pressed against me and hear the thunder of the growl starting deep in his body? The ghosts of the priest, choir, congregation, muted mutterings of a hundred prayers, massed voices of soaring hymns, ringing organ. Yes, indeed there were ghosts. I put the candles out before I left. I'm not sure whether I'll go back.

"I wish I could talk to Jerry about being lonely. No, what I mean is, I wish he understood. I can, and do, talk to Jerry about a great many things, usually what we are going to do, not very often of what I did before, because remembering hurts. Perhaps remembering is what life is for, we live on memories and moments gone by. That makes my life equal to very little. No, I can't talk to Jerry about it. It's too personal."

But I can, and often do, stamp and scream and rage at the world it, even if it doesn't hear me, or even care.

"Well, I think it's time to stop recording tonight. I'll open something so I can eat and then I'll take Jerry for a walk."

And walking along the beach, I'll throw wide my arms and shout my loneliness to the cold, far stars.

Crossroads Blues

Hey, thanks! Been walking that road forever, breathing everyone's fumes and not one cared to stop for me. Damn thumb near enough aching from being stuck out so long and being ignored, too!

This is one fine car, I have to say. Nice. What's the music ... oh, OK, never mind. I can live with it.

What? What do I like? Blues. Old style blues. Let me tell you a story, then, how I got to be where I was when you picked me up, you being a damn fine person and all, let me tell you. You up for that?

Well, like I said, I like the blues and I had this ambition, you know? Man, did I ever want to sing the blues! You know, like the old 'uns, none of this wailing guitars and sobbing violins and screaming keyboards... anyone can make a blues song outta that. No, me and the old guitar, a voice and a song and a heartbreak, that's what I wanna do. Like Robert Johnson, like Blind Lemon Jefferson, like the Reverend Gary Davis ... they didn't need no backing, did they?

So there I was, sat in the park – 'cos the family done got sick of me plucking the same chords over and over and I got jokes like 'I didn't wake up this morning' and stuff like that – crooning to myself about lost loves and too much drink and roads that go on forever especially when you're walking them, when this guy strolls up to me. Smooth like, slicked back hair, slicked back clothes, come to think on it and shiny shoes like they just came out of the box but he walked like they were slippers. That shouted money to me; you gotta spend a lot of money to get new shoes that soft and well fitting. I just drooled over the shoes.

Yeah, I know, supposed to be the females who are shoeaholics, but I do like a good pair of shoes and I had ambitions, oh yes, to go buy me handmade soft leather shoes one of these days, when the right person finds me and promotes me and I sell records by the million ...

You gotta have a dream, aintcha?

And here he was, the dream, right in front of me.

'Cos this here guy says, in a voice as slicked back as his hair, 'you got something there, son, I'd like to hear more.' Before I could answer, he snaps open a silver box like you'd keep smokes in but thinner, you know what I mean? And out comes a smart piece of card, embossed with silver and all, wouldn'cha know. Record Producer it said. His name? Don't ask, I didn't see. When you want a recording more than you want the next breath, well, sort of, who sees names? You see what you wants to see. I saw Record Producer. My heart near enough stopped in its rhythm, that it did.

The funny thing is, now I think on it, he never got impatient, no shuffling of feet in those fine leather shoes, no sigh of impatience as I stilled my heart and my thinking and my sudden desire to gush madly all over the place which wouldn't have been good, now would it, who wants sycophantic gushing, I ask you...

So I got myself together and I said, calmly and quietly, like, 'thank you, sir. I would really appreciate a chance to show the world what I can do.'

'Oh you will,' he said, so quiet like I wasn't sure I heard him. Even more slicked back than before. I started to think he was all oil inside, he was that smooth, that liquid, that – do you know, the word gloopy comes to mind? Now why would that be, I wonder?

So we goes for a drink, he ordering some fancy cocktail the like of which I'd never heard nor seen before and man, having seen how it looked in the glass, all sort of fiery and wild and dark and menacing – now there's another odd thing, menacing? A drink? Well it was, and right glad I was I asked for a straight pint. I know where I am with beer. You can keep the fancy stuff. He tossed the drink back and went and got another. Then I got to look at him proper like for the first time.

You know how some people's eyes are so black they show nothing? No? Well, that was how his looked to me. Couldn't read a thing in them, not a thing. Worried me a bit but I kept thinking 'record producer' and tried to overlook the almost blank face, the expressionless eyes, the cut of a mouth – hardly any lips, you see – and concentrated on the oily slicked back voice, which was talking of demo discs, of expensive recording time for free, of introductions to top people, of air play and of money.

'What do you want of me?' I asked eventually. Nothing comes free, there's always a price.

'Ha, about time you asked that.' There was an edge to the voice that hadn't been there before. I sat up a bit and wondered why the change.

'Well ... nothing's free, is it, not really...'

'A wise person, for a change. You're right, friend, nothing is free. I don't want much of you, actually. I would ask that the first recording we make be out in the open, is all, with a hand held recorder. We can clean it up later, be assured of that, but I want real blues, dirty down low and gutsy blues, I want – you to come to the crossroads at midnight and sing for me.'

Do you know, I fell for it? How stupid is that? You can ask yourself that question as I did and get no answer. It was the oily voice, you see, which held glittering promises in its depth, bit like oil that's spilled shows up as a rainbow. That kind of thing.

Damn me if I didn't go. The crossroads he specified were miles from anywhere, my beat up old car only just made it before it coughed its last and expired in a heap of rust right there on the side of the road. I had just pulled over in time. I got out, guitar rescued from the back seat, song in my head and my mouth, and went over to the crossroads – where he was waiting.

I still didn't fall in with knowledge, you know. Even though I had his card in my pocket and wondered why he spelled Damon as Daemon.

He had this fancy recording thing in his hand. I felt pretty damn stupid, standing at a crossroads singing a blues about standing at a crossroads, a sort of interpretation of Robert Johnson's which I rather

56

liked, but then I got into the spirit of it, sang my heart out and all but made my fingers bleed on the guitar strings.

He said I did just fine; it was exactly what he wanted. He said he would get in touch with me. I said thanks, don't you want to write down my name and address and stuff? No, he said, I know where you live and he reeled off my address, my phone number, my mobile number, my security information ... man, it were scary, I tell you.

I ain't been the same since. Something's gone out of me. Now I don't believe in this soul thing, but there might be a grain of truth in it, since I sang that song and stood on that crossroads, I feel different.

Empty.

Did I hear from him again? No.

What am I doing hitching? Trying to get back to the crossroads to see if I can get it back, whatever 'it' is.

Not holding out a lot of hope but hey, thanks for the ride. This is one lonely old road when you have to walk it.

The crossroads are right here.

Don't fancy staying with me, do you?

Thought not.

Through A Glass Darkly

Are you ready to enter the world of inanity, of insanity, of surreal surroundings and startling scenarios? You have come this far, what is a little further to you right now? Come with me: I am ready: I am the magician.

See how I stand waiting, hands raised?

From my fingers flows a river of cash, catch it if you can; catch it and hold it. Watch as it turns to blood. Ask yourself, is this is a nightmare? Are you dream-walking or awake? Eyes can see that which is not there as much as that which is. Cameras do lie. Nothing is as it seems. The neighbor you like is a serial killer at night. The job you have is transient. The love you have is incidental.

***

Walk with me. No, listen not to the voices that call you to go this way and that, to enter this building and that, you know not the truth of what they say, what they offer, what will happen if you go… or would you prefer to find out?

I thought not.

But then again, not only cameras lie. I might be lying, too. Do you trust me?

Fool if you do.

Watch my hands – no, better not. The night might catch the blade and reveal all my secrets…

You think I jest?

Of course I do.

Not.

Screams are for the weak. You are not weak, are you? Could you stand to have me cut you –thus – and not scream?

So you are one of the weak. All right... I will remember that. No, the blood will not stop flowing, but it will leave the trail you might need to retrace your steps and escape from the world into which I lead you.

If you can.

The darkness is complete. I prefer it that way. I banned all light, all lightness; all that starry stuff. I can't stand it, I like the dark. Things hide in the dark which cannot hide in the light, things I like, things I prefer, things which scare and terrify and –

You shake, you poor helpless spineless thing, you shake and that is only at my words. What will happen when the true horrors reveal themselves?

Oh, of course you're right, if it is true dark you cannot see the blood trail you've left. How foolish of me not to realize that.

How foolish of you to accept my words when I said them...

What else did I say which confused you, oh weak one? The night might catch the blade? Well, is that not so? The darkest darkness can still reveal the flash of a blade, silver cuts black, does it not? Silver cut you and you are no more substantial than a paper thin shadow in this dark, dark night.

I drink your fear as I would an elixir of pure life.

59

***

Enter my world.

It is one of smoke and mirrors, vanishing people and the true depiction of the tarot card, the Hanged Man, in my world is truly hanged and will stay so for the duration of the illusion. I am sorry to say he will not be restored to life; some things I have to leave to higher authorities than myself to undertake and I know, because I asked, that they will not intervene. He stays hanged.

His loss.

My gain.

I got to drink his life essence even as it spilled into the darkness.

Oh I'm sorry; I forgot to mention he's hanging right before your face. Did you hurt yourself on his buttons? How careless and remiss of me. Did I sound sincere enough? I've been working on it but somehow… it doesn't sound right.

No matter. It is of nothing compared with what is to come. I trust I do not frighten you? Too late if I do: you consented to come with me, did you not?

Foolish child.

A protest? Whatever your age, compared with my life - which covers eons - you are a mere child. In both intellect and understanding of the darker side of life. You have a fascination with the dark side, you all do, but few take the steps you did, to enter my world. I could call you fool but that would be unfair, to fools. They are wiser than you in their madness for their world is complete and perfect, as they perceive it.

Watch then where you set your feet, I would not wish your oh-so-clean shoes to be contaminated with that which the corpses have left behind.

And beware the darkness which brushes your eyelids and your shivering lips and leaves you shuddering...

And the wailing, oh the wailing which will enter your very soul and not leave you.

Ever.

Ah, protest as much as you wish, it is too late for that. You chose a walk on the wild side, did you not?

And so we move on. That which you thought was real is not and that which you thought was an illusion is real. If you ever work out which is which, that is the day I give up this tiresome job and hand it over to you.

***

Have you thought much, my newfound friend, on those who live close to you? Here in the darkness that is my soul and your destiny, you will have time for such esoteric thoughts. Trust me, I know it well.

That spiteful faced bitch – forgive me – who resides two doors away from you, the one who endlessly and everlastingly twitches the nets at her windows, the better to observe the comings and the goings... in this instance, the goings for I doubt much that you will return... do you know what she does -0h I am sorry, what she did - in the long distance darkness of the nights? Did you know of

61

those who called at the back door seeking favours that the younger ones would never give? The old, the desperate, the insane, oh how they come calling and the money flowed from the fingers to the pockets, a veritable river of cash. You ask, oh yes, of course I mentioned that which turns to a river of blood. She caught the river of cash all right. Did you know that she also fell into a river of blood? You did not? Where then have you been, or should I not ask such things? One of the – I must be polite here – customers... I need say no more.

And the smart gentleman, I can use no other word for him than that, he with the tie and the waistcoat and the gold chain and the smart peeping handkerchief from the top pocket, oh the elegance, long have I aspired to emulate such a thing! Did you know that –

Well, let me say, did you know that the neighbor who you like and I know well that you liked him, was a serial killer and that he ended his reign of terror with the spiteful faced bitch two doors away and left her in the river of blood.

Know well that when a body releases all its blood, it can indeed resemble a river.

I will demonstrate it to you when the time is right.

How many bodies? How many deaths? Over time, perhaps ten or more. And you never knew. How could you? He hid it behind his façade of excellence, of being the perfect English gentleman. What better mask could there be?

Apart from mine, of course. You do not know the real me. I fervently wish, for your sake, you never find out.

***

I have to ask your opinion on the employment situation as is seen by you in this world in which you once lived. Ha! You have noted the past tense – at last! I was beginning to think you had overlooked that small change. Insane? Of course I am. We all are. Aren't we? I admit, grudgingly, it is a matter of opinion.

I wish to talk, do you not understand? My life is – dull, empty, in need of constant stimulus. Talking is one such, it fills a small gap until the end, when I find true fulfilment.

Let us revert to the topic in mind. Employment. Do we need it, is it necessary, if you get it does it add anything to your life, enrich it in any way, or does it simply drag you down with the incessant demands of this 'higher than you in the food chain' person or that one? Days spent laboring over hot key incessantly clacking keyboards, watching often indecipherable codes sprawling across the screen, incomprehensible, impenetrable, uncomfortable in their superiority – 'we know what we are even if you do not' is the silent but all important message they convey to you in their complexity.

And as we stand here, in the all-encompassing darkness that is your soul, lightless and empty, you can look at that which you consider sustains you and see it for what it is – the transient illusion that

63

life will be better if you labour. Renounce such thoughts! Stand up for freedom! Refuse to go to work!

Or are you too cowed to do any more than follow the suit-clad sheep day by day by day onto the vehicles which will convey you to your destination? To endure a dust laden, emotion laden, spite-laden atmosphere where you are bound to be smilingly friendly to those you would not give a second glance to in the street?

And remember, employment is as fragile as a butterfly's wing. One sharp blast of cold commercial air and the damage is done, the 'company' folds, all are thrown out into the bitter reality of 'unemployment' for which read freedom, my friend, freedom from deadlines, overtime, politeness, tiredness, ulcers and worries. But I feel you do not agree.

Yet.

Darkness is good for the soul. It gives you your single opportunity to see that which is false and that which is real. Only reality glows in the dark.

***

That was indeed a hand. Severed neatly, I have to say with a sense of pride, severed very neatly indeed. No hacking there, one swift blow and the job was done.

Why? Because. Is there need to elaborate, to explain? If I consider a severed hand to be essential, if not critical, to my décor here, understand that it is my décor and I will add a severed hand to it if I so wish. No argument. I am the ruler here, I am the magician, remember? This domain is mine. As is the body from which I cleaved the hand.

No, I have not forgotten that you bleed. The wound is not deep but there is an unsustainable blood loss coming from it which will, if not treated, be your demise. I intended it that way. I have no means of bandaging the slashed limb. What I can say is, I will admire the patterned pathway you created by dropping your life essence on the floor as you walked. For that I thank you. A pleasure to come, to savour, to anticipate and to enjoy.

Now I wish to discuss that most fleeting, most ethereal, most damaging of emotions, love.

I spit as I say it. I reject it, scorn it, stamp on it and ban it from my domain. Love. It weakens a man, it twists his heart and mind; it makes him foolish, even as you were foolish enough to entrust me this night with your sanity.

Love is a four letter word. So is lust. Love is nothing more than lust with flowers and fancy perfumes as gifts. And you fall for it, time and time and time again. From earliest man in his cave, presenting his chosen beloved with wall paintings and dead mammoth to eat – and remember she had to cook the damn thing – to modern man aspiring to fly his beloved to somewhere exotic because it is expected of him, he ties himself down with a ring and a promise and then the chambermaid at the honeymoon hotel catches his eye with a sway of a hip and the bounce of a breast and he wonders why he ever got himself entrapped.

Where do you fit into that scenario, I wonder? A devoted long-time partner, a faithful spouse; an opportunist – shall we be crude for a moment? If willing totty is put before you, would you not take it?

Love is incidental to man. Lust is essential to man.

Be sure you know the difference.

Oh foolish me, I had quite forgotten you will not be returning home this night. You will not be there to see the circus that the forensics and police will create when they find the spiteful faced bitch in her river of blood, when they knock on your door and seek their answers, you will be missing and they will begin to wonder where it is you have gone and why you have gone, you who never go anywhere after dark for fear of being attacked.

And yet you walked into my snare. Some people have no sense.

I caution you, even as I lock this door and keep you on the inside of it whilst I walk free on the outside of it and go back to my life… the magician supervises your insanity as it takes hold.

Beware false illusions. Be aware that now no one can hear you scream.

A Little Piece of Home

Her hand trembled slightly as she reached for the flour jar. She told herself to stop being stupid, there was a loaf to be made and very little time in which to make it. She tipped the flour into the bowl and added the fat; her wrinkled fingers beginning the process of rubbing it in. If Gary were to walk in now, she thought, he'd say, as he always did: "You need a mixer, Gran, one with a dough hook. It'll do all that hard work for you. Go on, let me bring you Mother's." But she'd always made her bread this way and she always told him she was too told to change her ways.

The yeast smelled warm and friendly, the creamy-brown stream running wildly through and round the flour. She picked up the spoon and began to stir, her thoughts far away. Often she thought it must be wrong to love a child – a great-grandchild – like this. Gary was everything to her and he knew it; but unlike some people she could name, he had never taken advantage of the fact. She had loved him from the moment she first saw him, warm and pink, in the hospital cot. Joanna had been tired but happy; "what do you think of your first great-grandchild, Nan?" she'd asked. "We're calling him Gary."

"He's a lovely baby, dear."

She'd left the hospital with the picture in her head of the dark-haired, dark-eyed solemn baby who stared up at her and she knew this grandchild – this great-grandchild! – would be the love of her life, knew it with all the certainty of knowing she'd draw her next breath.

The dough flopped onto the floured worktop, the lengthy kneading process had begun. A montage of scenes and moments went through her mind along with the rocking turning movements of her hands …

Gary playing: "Going to the moon."

Gary at school: "I got a First in Science and Astronomy, Gran!" and the first ridiculous tinge of fear.

Christmas: "The rocket's my best present, Gran!" and she wondered why she'd bought it. The fear became a secret pain.

The teenager, broken hearted when his father died in Space: "Nothing will stop me going, nothing!" and the fear became an aching certainty.

She had watched the space-shot on television, the tiny, white-suited men walking across to the enormous rocket, made it all seem unreal. The man who waved to the cameras was not her Gary, not the child she remembered playing in her garden while she gossiped over tea with her granddaughter, not the boy who came proudly with his certificates to show her, seeking her approval more than the coin she gave him for reward. But a week in space is a long time when a moment, a hesitant breath, caused an accident and wiped out most of his family. The look he had when the grim news was broken was the same look he had when his father died; despair fighting with determination to go on.

She looked back and recalled to mind then the thought that there was nothing more life could do to hurt her. She buried her daughter and grand-daughter and nursed her badly wounded husband; all the time leaning on Gary for support until her husband finally gave up the fight and joined his daughter in the cold unyielding earth. But that pain had been a mere graze compared with the agony she was feeling now.

Kneading and folding, rocking and turning, the dough smoothed and firmed under her capable hands.

Gary had sat in her rocking chair in her tiny room, inside warm brick walls that had stood for so long it sometimes seemed as though time itself stood still in their comforting embrace. She looked at him; his face burned with the reflected light of a million stars, his eyes aglow with the wonders and mysteries of the darkness, the emptiness, the dreadful loneliness of space, and listened while he lied:

"It's just a job, Gran, like any other."

She dashed away a tear with the back of her veined hand and looked at the clock. Still five minutes to go before she could leave the dough to rise on its own. And still the unwanted memories flashed before her eyes.

Gary with a woman: "Meet the girl I love best in the world, Gran – after you, that is! This is Julia. She's an astronaut, too."

69

Flashing white teeth, glowing dark eyes and hair as ebony as the outer reaches of space itself... they would make beautiful children together, children she would never see. The tears fell unchecked and were kneaded into the dough, adding a touch of salt.

When Gary had come to tell her of his decision, a lifetime ago, he'd talked of things she could never understand; how he and Julia and their friends would be frozen and sent out into space to find a new planet, a new life. Just eight of them, suspended in time.

"Why couldn't you wait for me to die?" she'd shouted at him, selfish in her misery and despair and his eyes were pools of pain.

"I've waited, Gran, I've waited. I've tried to stay here on the ground, tried to settle for a life down here. I've let others go before me, you know I have! I can't let this chance go by, I was meant to lead, not to follow!"

"Your great-grandfather contented himself with his books and maps," she had sulked. "He lived out his dreams right here on Earth."

"Because you wouldn't go with him Gran," and the truth hurt. "He stayed because he loved you. If you'd gone with him, there wouldn't have been a place he wouldn't have visited... but you wouldn't go."

Then he'd gathered her frail body into his strong arms and hugged her.

"I can't stay, Gran, because I don't want to go to your funeral. I'm never going to buy a wreath and find my black tie for you. I want to remember

70

you as you are. When I wake up from my sleep, out there, I can think of you, baking, with the plates and jars all around you and I'll smell the yeast and think of home."

Selfish! Her mind had shouted. Selfish, not wanting to see me die is an excuse to go! But the words could not be said, nothing else could be said without destroying everything there was between them.

The young man looked at the old woman across the generations as the sky turned dark and teardrops sparkled on the blackness.

Even though it might risk everything, she had to have the last word. The prerogative of the old.

"My husband was happy, living out his earthbound dreams."

"And I couldn't be."

There was no answer, nothing that even in the depths of her wisdom and love could she find to answer his deep determination and logic.

She stopped kneading and smoothed the soft, resilient dough, pressing down with a fingertip and watching it spring back. A plait, she decided, a plait glazed and sprinkled with poppy seeds.

Today Gary was coming for the final goodbye and she would give him the loaf. One day, far beyond the reach of any imagination, he would wake from his frozen time-suspended sleep and there would be, for the sharing, a little piece of home.

Road Rage

Roads.

Hate them. Damn things just lie there on the ground, stretched out like pieces of black rubber bands or strips cut from tyres and laid there, held down with kerb stones each side or yellow lines or even, heaven forbid, grass because no one goes along there and cuts it, do they? Now why don't I think that a road with a grass edge is a real road?

What does it matter? I still hate them.

Well, listen up and I'll tell you why.

Cos the damn things go *somewhere* and *somewhere* ain't where I wanna go. Not any more, anyway.

Had the wanderlust, I did, itchy feet and all. Remember that silly song 'I was born under a wandering star'? That was me. Wanted to walk the world, I did, I saw what it looked like in China, Malaysia, Peru, any of them African countries, any of them Arab countries, wanted to see what made the Arctic different from the Antarctic or were the road signs the same in both places, thick with ice and covered in snow and unreadable...

Joke.

Sorry.

Anyway – got the picture? Wandering me? Left the family a long, long time back, 'cos they didn't want to go wandering, they wanted to sit by the fireside with the dog and the cat and the vegetables in the garden and the thatched roof full of birds and twitters and creepy things that rustled

72

the strands at night and scared the **** out of me. They're welcome to it, I thought, being all of seventeen, all growed up and knowing what I wanted. I thought.

Surprising how wrong you can be, ain't it?

So what I did for a while was, went walking miles and miles, sleeping by roadsides, ear to the ground, hearing the thrum of the lorries, oh man, you could hear them coming for miles, them great wheels pounding the surface and shaking the earth and then going by with a roar and a whoooooosh of wind so sharp and hard it could have you clean off your feet. And gone on to the next village, next town; next city. How come I never stuck out a thumb and got me a ride is the question I am busy asking right now. With no answer, unless it be that I needed to walk it myself, every step, even when dogged tired and feet so sore they could hardly stand the weight of me anymore. Talking of that, I lost so much weight I looked like a wraith, or so me Ma said when I went back. Least, I think she said wraith, she might have said rake, come to think on it. Not that it matters, either way I was as thin as one of them reeds thatching our cottage. And come to think on it again, I was fit to rustle like one of them, too, when –

But I ain't there yet.

I'm here. Like here. On the side of the road. Learning to live with the sound of the cars and the lorries and learning which was which, even by the engine and the thrum of the wheels. Oh my, I do like that expression, don't I?

73

You see, I never learned much in my life up to then, so I set myself the job of learning the difference and it worked and it felt good and I thought – hey, I can do sommat now that perhaps no other person can do! Oh that felt good. I mean, I ain't much good otherwise, am I?

What?

You know that song, "King Of The Road", yes, another song, grew up with songs, could tell you a hundred songs that fit this story, "Road To Hell" is one ... no, that old king of the road song, where he sweeps a floor and things like that. That was me. That was me labouring here and there, fix a gate for someone, muck out the stables for someone else, chop firewood, pluck a chicken, you be surprised how many people want sommat done if you just ask right and don't ask for money. I never did ask for money, never had any either. I got food and a night's shelter and sometimes someone took pity on me and would give me fresh jeans or shirt or a jacket that had a tear here or there but was just fine by me. Oh and a hat to keep the sun off. Suited me just fine.

I did that for what seemed like forever. Enjoyed it no end. Met all sorts of people, learned the good from the bad from the indifferent and the downright mean.

Then I met him.

Hold on. That should be Him.

I was walking this road, see, leaving the lorries and trucks and hauliers to themselves for a while, travelling a back road to see what it felt like. Different, I gotta give you that. Saw a fox or two, all sorts of scurrying things – didn't know what they were, what's the difference between a shrew and a dormouse and a field mouse and a –

Anyway, wild flowers and wild animals and good sunshine and then I realised, in a moment, that someone was walking with me.

There was no one there a breath before, I swear on my reputation, such as it be, as an honest individual. Then he was there. Dark face, dark eyes, dark thoughts and all.

"Do you mind if I share your journey?"

Like he was dressed for it, mind. Sharp suit and white shirt, blue tie crossed with gold lines, smart as you like, complete with polished lace up shoes. Not your usual kit for tramping the road, is it?

But I was brought up proper and even if I had a pretty cute idea of who he was, I said, nice as you like: "You're most welcome."

He hardly seemed to draw breath, was busy talking to me about roads, how they went somewhere and that somewhere was usually more interesting, or so we thought, than the place we had just left, when in truth all places were the same.

"No, they're not," I said when he paused for a moment in his discourse. "The people may look the same, but they ain't."

"Interchangeable, my friend, that's what they are." Then he stopped and looked at me. "You know who I am, don't you?"

"I do."

"And you haven't asked me for anything."

"Why should I? Got all I want outta life."

75

He frowned. "This isn't right. Everyone wants something."

"I don't."

"Not fame, wealth, women?"

Laughter consumed me for a moment. "Fame, me? Got the intelligence of a flea, who's gonna make me famous? Money? Got all I need. Women? You can keep them, nothing but trouble, they be."

"A wise person. I would pick a wise person for today's Good Deed, wouldn't I?"

We were walking again by then, step by step nearer some little town that I had never seen before and would never see again once I passed through, following the road to wherever it led me.

"Well, I suggest you move on and give someone else a Good Deed for the day, sir. I am content with my walking, thank you. Oh, and thank you for your company for this while, too."

His eyebrows went up. "You mean it, don't you? More and more surprising. I cannot go without leaving you a gift, my friend. One that has no strings attached whatsoever. I will make you a telepath. Then you can use the power of your mind to get what you need when you need it, be it food, clothes or shelter."

It sounded good to me, so I said thanks and he – disappeared. I walked on, content.

And then my problems began.

It was a double edged gift indeed. Oh yes, I could use my power to get what I wanted all right, I had food, clothes, shelter aplenty.

76

I also knew just what those people thought of me. I had their thoughts coming at me, theirs and everyone else's too. It was as if every person was speaking aloud all the time and I could hear everything.

"Here comes a tramp, hide everything afore he steals it."

"Damn cadgers coming in here, wanting sommat for nothing."

"Suppose we'd better give him a job, send him on his way, he can have that meat, it's been off a couple of days but who cares, he'll be long gone by then."

And the other thoughts:

"I hate him, I wish him dead, I hate him and I want him dead..."

"Could throw her down and do it, couldn't I? What could she say, big man like me..."

"Not enough money to buy food, what am I going to do..."

Every thought, every mood, every variation on every human misery there is.

It battered me, it haunted me; it revolted me. You would not believe what thoughts people hide behind smiling faces. Or perhaps you would, if you've been around long enough to know the true heart of man.

I couldn't stand it.

I went back to where I met him, called to him to take his gift back, begged on my knees for my peaceful existence once more – and then I realised what I had done.

I had scorned a gift from the Devil. He had got his own back in such a subtle way that no one could accuse him of being vindictive.

I also realised it wasn't going to go away.

So I braved the town, as it were, got myself some money, bought myself a load of supplies I thought I would need and some I didn't but have sure come in handy and I left the road, climbed up the mountainside and occupied a cave where I live now. The only thoughts I get up there are birds and animals and they don't bother me none.

I venture down occasionally, brave the battering of the townsfolk, buy more supplies, get my beard and hair cut and get back up out of the way. And there I'll stay until God or the Devil calls me home.

Well now, I better be off. You're thinking you ain't heard such a load of baloney in a long time, right? I see by your face you were disbelieving and now you have to believe 'cos I nailed it, didn't I, everything you were thinking about me.

I'm going back up there, to my cave, where the thoughts are pure and the air is clean and I stay off them roads.

Guess you could call it road rage, of a kind.

It ain't, but with the Devil you don't win. There's them as would have took and took and me, who wanted nothing, got something anyway.

D'you know, thinking on it, I didn't get too bad a deal, did I? I don't walk them endless black strips anymore and I don't have much to do with them there townsfolk and don't that just do me fine?

Just don't let him know where I am, in case he comes a-looking for me with another gift. If that happened, you might find out what road rage is really like.

Cos he won't let me off so easy next time.

I Will Wait For You

The City of London, ancient as the ground it stands on, modern as the towering, strange buildings it has seemingly manufactured out of nothing, has more than its share of graveyards.

The worker and casual visitor to the Square Mile, where money changes hands at an alarming rate, where fortunes are made and lost, where the Bank of England sits like the old lady she has been likened to and holds on to the riches she has acquired over the countless years of being in the centre of the Square Mile of commerce, are not always aware of them.

Most cities never sleep, but this one does. This one closes down at night, leaving the rats and strays to haunt the narrow alleyways, the wide affluent streets, the banks of the great never sleeping river Thames. The vagrants shuffle into marked chosen doorways with their newspaper blankets and cardboard walls, which they zealously and jealously guard, newspapers, cardboard and doorways, that is, to settle down for the night, so much litter swept to one side, so much misery wrapped in paper and tied with string.

In Temple, haunt of barristers and clerks and worried litigants, the gas lamps sing their litany of warmth and light to nothing but empty courtyards and silent Chambers. The drinking place alongside the great City church lets its lamps invite in those who have money to buy their way to oblivion, if that be their wish, but who close early most nights for lack of custom.

Into that strange half-haunted world come the non-people.

The City, graveyards, buried rivers and deep sewers once worked in by men called toshers who searched the murky disgusting depths for money, rags, bones and any other treasures that could be found, is a natural place for the non-people to live. Their homes have long since been disturbed, their memorials left leaning against walls or built into the walls themselves, a token nod to their memory. They come seeking revenge and retribution and remembrance.

It is surprising how few know that the bodysnatchers plied their trade there, resurrecting corpses for the anatomists in the great City hospitals, especially Barts.

Few know that among those who called themselves non-people are those who live on blood. Non-people who take on the cloak of humans in order to get what they want and need. Humans that are mostly ignored or scorned.

Those who trespass into the City at night find this out at their cost – the ultimate cost, their lives.

The night was drawing in when Karl stumbled into the City from the West End, drunk, heartbroken and lost. He had one thing left in his pocket, the ring his bride-to-be had thrown in his face during a bitter argument in St James's Park. She had stormed off in one direction; he had stormed off in the other direction and sought consolation for his sorrows in the nearest pub. He then ended up walking without realising or even caring where he went. The words they had thrown at one another over some stupid, infinitesimally small item were of such bitterness and ferocity it was clear they could never speak to one another again. Somewhere in his drunken stupor, Karl realised that it was not the item which had caused the row but long built up tensions which had finally exploded. Better before the wedding than after, he tried to console himself.

It didn't work.

The City was quiet, only his heels disturbed the night as he stomped his way down Cheapside, heading for who knew where? Alone in a city of towering heartless buildings, shuttered and barred for the night, offices which held the secrets of millions of people in its archives and databases, vaults which held wealth beyond belief, especially those of the jewellers in Hatton Garden – ah, if he only had the skills to break in, to handle the beautiful gems and elegant pieces, if only, if only...

In a moment he was stone cold sober. The ring in his pocket seemed to be burning its way through the cloth, heating his skin. He pulled it out and went to throw it, but stopped. The diamond was worth something, the gold was worth something, why throw it away? Why not choose someone worthy of having it as a gift ... one of these vagrants, stinking and snoring in a doorway? Why not be truly magnanimous and give the gift of a lifetime to someone, change their future forever? Well, perhaps that was going a little too far but still...

He had no need of it. He could not bring himself to walk into a jewellers and sell it, for they would know what had happened and pride, that all enveloping sin, would not let him do that, not allow someone to smile sympathetically and wish him better luck next time. Best to give it away and start over again – if there was a next time.

But which one of the human flotsam could he give it to, why was one more deserving than another?

Random luck, he told himself, like winning the lottery, sometimes they draw the lucky number, the rest of the time, for some, the rest of their lives, they don't.

He stopped by a particularly savage looking drunk, long grey hair tied back with string, huge shaggy beard, incredibly lined face and gnarled twisted hands clutching the newspaper tightly to his body. The night was not cold, but habit dies hard.

'Hey you!' Karl nudged the sleeping man with his highly polished shoe, provoking a grunt that could have been 'clearorff' or something vulgar. He couldn't quite make out the words. He tried again. 'Look, I've got something for you.'

The eyes flicked open and for a moment Karl felt intense fear for they were black and soulless. Then the man blinked and the face changed.

'What'd'r'yer want then? I was kipping.'

'I want to give you something. I don't want it any more, it's worth a lot of money and I chose you to give it to.'

'What is it?'

'This.'

Karl held out the ring and the man took it, suspiciously turning it every way he could.

'What's the catch?'

'No catch. I broke up with my fiancé and that's it, end of relationship. I don't want to sell the ring, I want to give it to someone else to sell.'

'No one gives someone sommat for nuffink. What do you want me to do for it?'

'Nothing.' Karl was beginning to despair; the man was not grateful, just suspicious. 'Look, it's not stolen or anything, just take it and in the morning see if you can trade it for money to help you live.'

'Now who's gonna believe I got this legit?'

Karl was baffled. It was something he hadn't thought of, not for a moment. Of course, how could someone looking and smelling like that walk into a jeweller's and trade the ring for cash?

He made up his mind in that moment. 'All right. I'll remember you. I'll be back in the morning. I'll sell the ring myself and bring you the money.'

The teeth were stained and black but they still showed themselves in a grim smile. The vagrant grabbed Karl's arm in a tight vicious grip. 'I'll wait for you.'

'I will be back.'

'Don't you go ratting on me. You don't promise me a lifeline and then rat on me. I'll wait for you.'

Nodding, Karl stuffed the ring back in his pocket and walked swiftly away. He knew the doorway he knew the man, he would return.

He thought.

Taxis disappear at night from the City, for there are no passengers to hail them and be taken to distant destinations. The taxi drivers can make a killing by driving by theatres and nightclubs instead. Karl knew he would have to get the Underground to go home. Mansion House, perhaps? But his footsteps were not taking him to an Underground station. He didn't quite know where he was going, it seemed drink and sorrow were combining to send him wandering aimlessly down narrow streets that held menace in every darkened window and doorway, taunted him with glimpses of civilisation, street lights and occasional cars, but he could not quite make his way to them.

He stumbled into what he thought was a small park, until he saw the gravestones around the walls. Oh what the hell, he thought, I'll just...

The morning sun touched his red rimmed eyes and woke him. Dishevelled and hung over, he somehow staggered to his feet, trying to brush dirt and early morning dew from his once fine suit. His throat was raw and his stomach screamed for something, anything, to stop the sick feeling which was consuming him. Too late, it had to come out.

'Sorry,' he muttered to whoever the headstone commemorated. 'You know how it is...'

He reached for a handkerchief and realised the pocket was empty. The ring had gone. Somewhere in the dark hours someone had robbed him, his wallet, his watch and the ring had gone.

'NO!' he roared into the silent morning, startling the birds into frantic squawking song in the trees. 'NO!' Fear gripped him, turning him to ice. He saw the soulless eyes of the vagrant, heard the menace in the voice, 'I will wait for you.' A voice that in that moment was not that of a vagrant drunk, but a cultured being, one with strength, one with purpose ... one who meant what he said.

I have to go and explain...

Was that not foolish? A sane voice in his head questioned the decision. The man knows not who you are. Go home. Walk if you must. Report the theft to the police at least, get them to take you home. Forget the vagrant.

'I will wait for you.'

He couldn't. Something was drawing him back to the doorway, to the man whose life he promised to change – and would dismally fail to do so.

Somehow he got himself moving; somehow he knew he had to find his way back. He had no idea where he was, but he thought if he let his subconscious work out the direction, he would be there in no time, not like the meandering aimless walk he had taken the night before. That was nothing but a jumbled memory anyway.

The sour taste of vomit in his mouth, hair awry and clothes wrecked, Karl staggered into the street and began to walk, letting his feet take him where they would.

And sure enough he was heading back to the building he remembered. And sure enough the vagrant was there, sitting up, alert, anticipating.

'Too damn early for you to have sold the ring,' he growled as Karl walked up to him. 'And you look like sommat the dog brought in from the dump.'

'I ... fell asleep in a graveyard last night and someone robbed me.'

'Right. Good story. Some ghoul came out of his grave and took the ring, did he?'

'Ring, wallet, watch, everything.'

The vagrant began to laugh. 'Right, mister, like I believe that story. Going back on your promise, then, are you?'

'I can't – I need to go home. I can find money and bring it back to you. I promise!'

The man stood up, towering over Karl. He had not appreciated how tall the man was, curled up in the doorway he looked small, almost insignificant. Now he revealed himself as over six foot and broad with it. The fear Karl had experienced in the graveyard was nothing to what he felt in that moment.

'You know what the old highwaymen used'ta say, dontcha? Your money or your life. You tell me you got no money, so – '

Karl's lifeless, bloodless body lay in the doorway for several hours before someone found him and reported the death to the police. The autopsy revealed not a drop of blood remained in his veins.

Back Where I Belong

It's dark in here. Too dark for me to see anything. I'm restricted in my movements, why can't I sit up, move my arms about, lift my head... and what 's this strange silky stuff I'm lying on? What's this hard pillow I'm resting on...

I don't like this. Any of it. Not one single tiny, miniscule scrap of it. Something's wrong and I want to know where and why and how and what and I want to know now. Not tomorrow, or next week, or next year, but NOW!

TALK TO ME!

Nothing. It's as if I'm in some kind of box...

I am, aren't I, in some kind of box. A coffin, to be precise.

What else is lined with silky stuff and holds my arms and legs and body in a rigid position where I can't move around and...

But I'm not dead!

Hold on, think this one through. Sensibly, logically, one step at a time.

I was...

Where?

In my car. Right. First step, in my car. Driving from/to?

Work. I remember. Driving from work, after a long day. Tired. Trying to keep my eyes open. Remember... some idiot cutting in front of me and me too tired to react quickly and I smashed into him. I remember nothing else.

So, did someone declare me DOA? If so, I've been a long time waking up, there would have been an autopsy – hold on – can I feel – yes I can – and then a funeral and they don't happen very quickly and –

I guess I got buried, because I'm not burned up and ash and scattered somewhere or left in the bottom of the incinerator or stuffed into someone else's urn.

But you see, I'm NOT dead.

I need to get out of here. So, how do I get out of a) the coffin and b) the grave...

By sheer hard work.

Wow, that was hard work too!

Oh hell. I've been dead longer than I thought. The headstone's in place already. No, not already, look at the date, look at the date ... I've been dead a year. A whole long empty wasted do-nothing year.

But I look all right, what I can see of me, anyway. Not much rotting going on here, feet still got shoes on and nothing leaking out of the seams. The socks don't feel soggy either, so... the feet must be intact. Right? The legs, let me look at the legs, tug up the trousers, well, would you look at that, pink flesh and blue veins and come to think of it, what about the hands which did the tugging? Well, would you look at that, too, all my fingers intact and heavens, she buried me with my wedding ring, too! I thought she would have had that off me and sold it immediately. Or do I do my cheating wife an injustice...?

Right. Head. Hmm, seems intact. Eyes, yes, nose, definitely, mouth with teeth, yes, and at least now I can say I will never have toothache again, hallelujah! Ears? Yes, I have ears. Hair? Longer than I normally have it but who's arguing about a small item like that?

Looks me as if I am pretty well intact. Not bad for my age, as it happens. My age plus one year – obviously lying around underground does wonders for the body. Look, no paunch. That's the death starvation diet for you, works every time. I might market that, when I get myself back into civilisation.

And the bitch's house.

Now, let me orientate myself.

This is the large new burying ground, so my home is – several miles away. Well, I obviously can't drive there and equally can't hire a taxi either; there's no money in these pockets.

Hold on, you fool, you're not thinking straight.

Would you, after a year underground? Asleep?

No excuse. Come on, think! How did you get out of the coffin and the grave?

By thought.

Precisely.

Now think yourself at home.

Ha! Is it that easy, I ask myself... there's only one way to find out... isn't there?

And here I am walking up the path. She's made a few changes, that black-hearted wife of mine. The flower beds are all shrubs, no colour, no charm. Where's the central rose bush gone? Pride of my life, that was. What's a conifer doing in its place?

The door's a different colour. I preferred the green; don't like this – this wishy washy blue. That's not a colour for a front door, that doesn't say 'look at me, I am proud to be the entrance to this home.' This one says, 'I am all delicate pastels and femininity and be kind to me.'

I will, when I get in.

Sudden thought, no one appears to have seen me yet. Was I lucky or am I invisible? I will find out when I-

Shocked look, smashed dishes, hand over mouth, eyes like saucers – I thought that was a stupid expression until I saw her eyes go as big as saucers when I walked into the (disgustingly yellow) kitchen.

'You...'

'Me.' I don't think I have a voice, leastways I didn't hear anything. Telepathy, perhaps, because her eyes got even bigger, if that was possible and it had to be, because they did.

Stop it with the foolish thoughts.

'It is you.' She's shaking head to foot, nerves, fright, love? Never the last one, never, never. I know my wife and a lot of memories are creeping back. Well, I've only been out of the grave for – how long? Half an hour? Taking me a little while to get myself together. Only natural.

Let's think about the reason I was so tired and couldn't react properly in the accident. Let's think about the flask she gave me to take to work, the drink which tasted just the tiny bit wrong, think about the look of sex she carried from time to time when she hadn't been with me. Think about the lies

91

... oh the lies ... I uncovered from time to time without her knowing.

Think about how she'll react when I say the next words to her.

And smile.

'Darling, I got tired of lying in the grave. I decided to come back where I belong.'

Burning Love

"How much do you hate him?"

The words seemed to shock the young man. He pushed his tousled hair back with one hand, an obvious time wasting exercise to give him a moment to think before responding. Shock gave way to a glimmer of understanding.

"As much as you."

I laughed, showing him white teeth set amid blood red lips and tongue. No matter his apparent exhaustion, he still twitched. I saw it.

"You can't, my beloved, you can't. I hate him with every fibre of my being and no one can hate more than that."

"Janetta, my darling..." He reached for me but I rolled away, savouring the smell of crushed grass as I did so. Nature at its most basic. Grass crushed beneath a human body.

"Enough, enough! You were wonderful, you are wonderful, my joy, my heart, my life, but no more tonight. I need to think..."

"We've made our plans."

"Randy, you made plans, I'm not sure we can go with them just yet."

I pushed myself over onto my back, gazing up at the velvet night sky, wondering how many stars there were and whether anyone had succeeded in counting them. The thought that each one was a fireball intrigued me, as fire itself intrigued me, the colours, the flickering of the flames, the greed with which it consumed whatever it could find, wood, coal, paper, cloth, flesh, hair, bones...

Those thoughts were best kept very secret indeed. I had Randy where I wanted him, to some degree, but not enough to let him in on my thoughts and dreams and ambitions. Somewhere an owl hooted, close by the undergrowth rustled and I caught sight of a fox loping quietly away, mouth open so it had caught nothing – so far. Well, that makes two of us, my friend, I mused and laughed silently.

"I'm getting cold." Randy got up and began swinging his arms around to generate some heat. Reluctantly I got up, without his help. Lithe and sinuous as I am, I could get myself up from the ground without assistance. It was something he said he admired, my independence, which translated to my inability to accept help. I thought it was a drawback; there were times when a little help would not come amiss.

"I'm going home," I announced with an edge on my voice that said, 'no argument.' Randy nodded, a movement I could just about see in the darkness caused by the huge oak.

"Then let's go."

We walked along the edge of the cornfield, the ears ripe and ready for harvest, the wind stirring them so they spoke in sibilant whispers to one another. I wondered if anyone could speak the language of the corn and if they could, what they would learn. Then I berated myself for stupid thoughts. Hold on to reality, I told myself. There is one big thing to do and the sooner you do it, the better.

Randy left me at the steps leading up to the house. He walked off without once looking back, just as I had told him to do, so why the tinge of disappointment that he hadn't turned round once to look at me? What good was a lover if they didn't act like one? Even if it meant breaking the rules I had given him ... but then, had I not chosen him because he was compliant, meek and obedient?

I hurried up the steps, my footfall silent in expensive leather pumps. The door eased open without a sound and I slipped through the gap, all but holding my breath. There was no member of staff around that I could see. With a sigh of relief I climbed the stairs to my room, where I locked the door behind me and threw myself on the bed, only then realising I had been actually been holding my breath all the way up.

Hate.

An all-consuming emotion that blinds people to reality, reasonable thought, often reasonable behaviour. Hate. Hatred. Loathing. Detestation. Whatever the name, whatever the word, the object of that hate became unbearable.

And Stuart Edward Philip De Vere Walston, my husband of ten years and three days, if I was counting – which I surely was – had become unbearable to my vision, my hearing and my touch. His voice grated on me, his platitudes were a patronising condescension – if I could phrase it thus – and all I wanted, dreamed of, visualised over and over, was plunging a sharpened steak knife into his starched shirt front, seeing the richness spill out and stain the white and then the black of his ubiquitous evening suit. The problem: that vision was swiftly accompanied by the one of the police arriving, arresting me and taking me away in handcuffs, incarcerating me in some ghastly prison cell for years and years.

Even hate has a price, a step it is impossible to take for the sake of sanity.

Oh, but there are other ways to wreak revenge.

I sat up, reached for a cigarette and then remembered I had quit smoking a week earlier. No, that was the wrong term; I had decided to delay having a cigarette. The 'delay' had now gone on for just over a week and it was getting easier, although I missed the feel of the slender tobacco packed tube in my fingers, the flare of the lighter, the flame which brought instant relaxation and pleasure. Ignore the ash, the tainted breath, the smelly clothes, the tarred lungs...

Stop it, I told herself. Stop it! Anyone can do diversionary tactics like that.

Face facts.

My husband, the local squire, land owner, Master of the Hunt, benefactor to the local community, is a two timing nasty piece of work.

Clothes stop people from noticing the bruises from the vicious pinches or sly jabs with an elbow, hard enough to damage.

He thinks I don't know about his dalliances, his one night stands, his longer term affairs, thinks I can't see or don't see the looks he gives the current one who has caught his attention, someone who will be bought off when he's bored, in about three weeks, judging by the rate he gets through them.

And I get Randy, a farm hand, a rough and ready labourer. The thing is, Randy is always ready and if he is sometimes rough, it doesn't matter.

Randy professes to hate my husband as much as I do. I disbelieve him for his home, where he and his older brother still live, is owned by the farm and by my husband. His job is dependent on my husband. He can tell me he hates him but I disbelieve him and know that, apart from me, no one hates him for no one sees him as I do. But he's useful, he's discreet, he's young, he has staying power and he's good looking. And in awe of me. What more could I ask?

Well, peace of mind for one.

How to get it is something else.

I'm not letting my husband continue to get away with endless affairs, which he flaunts in front of me, knowing full well I am aware of them. Is it my fault he scorns my room and my bed? Is it my fault I am no longer the young woman he courted and married? Does it not occur to him that he too is ten years older and sagging in places?

I know what I want to do. I know it well enough that I can see it happening and, with the right circumstances, no one will know anything about it until it is over. None of this hacking at his chest with a steak knife and having witnesses to the act. No, nothing as crude as that.

Hit him where it hurts. In the bank account.

All I have to do is work out the very best way of doing it...

I was the model wife for weeks. Entertaining guests, running the house, supervising the perfect meals, I did nothing that he could criticise in any way, shape or form. He did not visit my room, for which I was grateful, for I would have found it difficult to respond with enough ardour to satisfy him. That I saved for Randy and nights on the edge of the cornfield, with the rustling sound of the corn talking to itself as background to my cries of passion.

It was then the seed of an idea came to me.

The first task was to find out where my husband conducted his dalliances with his latest paramour. Slut, whore, two timing friend... the names could go on forever but were futile, he had power, money and status, she had ambitions and that I understood. My revenge was not going to be against someone he had managed to entrap, but against him, the monster, the ogre, the bane of my days and my existence.

I bribed a stable lad to follow them one night, to find out where they went when she visited our estate. Simple, he said, they were so engrossed in one another they had no idea he was following. They went to a small cottage on the outskirts of the land, one I had seen many times when out riding but ignored. It was tumbledown, in drastic need of renovation and repair and I never thought about why recently the roof had been patched, the windows replaced, the door shutting properly. Foolish woman that I am, I thought perhaps he planned to put a tenant in there. Instead he was using it to put a part of him into her. I wondered what it was like inside the cottage, how much effort he had made, without actually wanting to find out. Mixed up feelings fighting for precedence and none of them winning.

He spoke at dinner about the money we would reap – I use the word advisedly – when the harvest was gathered in, mentioned the high price of corn, the heavy crop we had raised this year together with the barley and the wheat. He spoke of a new carriage, we could afford it, he said, when it was sold and the money banked safely. I sat and listened and nodded and said 'yes' in the right places and smiled at him as if delighted with the fact we could have a new carriage and money in the bank, as if that made up for his philandering right before my eyes. I saw nothing but my need for revenge. I ask now, do you blame me? Have not countless women – and men, come to that – felt the same over the centuries, when they find the love of their life has been dallying with someone else? My problem was, he had not been the love of my life in the first place, but he was my husband, the fact I didn't care about him was immaterial. Possession is everything. He chose me before he chose them. Illogical, I know, but to me it was perfect feminine reasoning.

I chose a night when Randy was full on ready in every sense of the word. We met at our trysting place, the base of the oak, where undergrowth had created its own enclosure. We met and we loved intensely for some time. Then I complained I really needed a cigarette and pulled the box of matches from my pocket. Randy laughed; he had never seen me smoke and could not believe I did, or that I owned such things. I had a cigarette with me but had no intention of lighting it. Instead I struck the match, missed the cigarette, to his amusement, and threw the lighted match onto the patch of fuel I had carefully dropped in the corn an hour or so before we met.

It was spectacular. An entire cornfield went up in flames in no time at all, the corn no longer whispered, it shrieked in its dying throes. At least, that is what I heard, the dying of the corn. I could almost hear my husband shrieking at the loss of income from the harvest.

It was only when the flames had died down that the source of the shrieks was discovered. Instead of using the cottage that night, he and his paramour had chosen a place in the corn.

I had my witness in Randy who swore that I had thrown a match away that I shook to extinguish the flame before I threw it. I had the staff who spoke of my husband's dalliances with all and sundry and how he normally used the cottage but this night had seemingly changed his mind.

Revenge is a dish best served cold? No, revenge comes in flickering flames, intense heat and the sure knowledge that the memories will live with you forever.

I ask you, how many women get to burn down a cornfield – and their cheating husband with it?

The corn has grown again and it whispers its secrets. I am grateful no one understands the language that it speaks.

Inspired by Randy Newman's Let's Burn Down the Cornfield

Autumn Leaves

Ellie studied the pattern made by the golden leaves which had drifted from the multitude of twigs and branches on the ancient horse chestnut trees. Ever year Nature created a carpet to walk on, every year the pattern was completely different, yet no one seemed to notice, no one seemed to appreciate the talent, the artistic flair shown by the different designs.

Autumn leaves. In Autumn everyone leaves. She shivered as a cold breeze played with her hair and tinged her cheeks with colour. Everyone leaves. In Autumn her father had left, walked out of the door to go to work and never came back. Left them bemused and concerned; then afraid and finally desperately lonely. No police ever came to report a body; no visitor mentioned his not being there. It was as if he had never been. Like Autumn leaves, he had come and gone and few had mourned his passing. Ellie remembered the aching loneliness more than the sorrow, if she had experienced that emotion at all. She had no idea how her mother felt. Nothing was ever said.

Her brother had left in the Autumn with a back pack of books, writing pads, pens, pencils, all the paraphernalia imaginable to study. Virtually no clothes, she recalled; only books and writing things. She had commented on it at the time and had nothing in return but raised eyebrows and a look which said, 'don't be stupid.' So she didn't. She let him walk away to University without so much as a hug or a kiss on the cheek or a wish for his future. She had not been on his wavelength at any time during their joint lives; a goodbye would not have made any difference to the way she felt.

They were two then, two people in a house made and furnished for four. Two people who managed to avoid speaking about the things which mattered, the way they felt, the loneliness they endured, the hollow holes in their lives, but instead spoke of late mail delivery, the quality of the food in the local supermarket, the fact that next door were playing their music loud again, even though they had complained. Several times, in fact. Trivial talk. Light talk. As light, as ephemeral as the Autumn leaves which fell, rotted, became one with the earth and enriched it. Their talk would not enrich anything, it added nothing to their lives, to their understanding of life and how to live it, their need to overcome their inhibitions and talk of pain and hurt and suffering and emptiness.

Autumn was an aching time of sadness, melancholia, withdrawal; the windows full of Halloween trivia, as trivial as the talk which sometimes passed for companionship. Autumn was a time of sharp frosts, rich scents of bonfires, of fruit, the true Harvest Home, the season of richness and of ending. Autumn was a time of dying.

Her mother had died in the Autumn. One day she had sat down in a chair, complained of not feeling well, touched her head theatrically as if in a silent movie melodrama – and stopped breathing. Ellie had, for the longest time, done nothing. She had watched the life empty out of a body and depart and she stood and did nothing. Did not dare to touch the hand, the arm, the shoulder or the face for fear of drawing the life back. She knew, without being told, that the life had wanted to go, that since her father had walked out of the door and not returned, life had become as melancholy as the season itself, but lasted all year. Only when she grew stiff and her legs ached with standing did she move to the telephone and dial the local surgery, repeating the information to the bored hassled impatient receptionist. Yes, she would wait for the doctor to come. Yes, she would wait for a call. No, it was not a problem.

Only then did she sit down, tucking her feet under the chair, hands in her lap and stared at the person she had called mother but for whom she had no affection whatsoever. Somehow that had dried up, fallen from the branch of family life she represented, drifted to the ground and become compost which, sadly, had produced nothing. At least the Autumn leaves produced fungi and new shoots for wild creatures to sustain themselves. Ellie felt she had been unsustained for many years.

When the men came and took the body away, leaving her with nothing but memories, Ellie blinked a few times, looked around the room and began to catalogue in her mind what she would keep and what had to go. There was much to do, so many decisions to make to do, but she did nothing but look around the room and make decisions. That would go to the charity shop, that would go to the antique dealer, that would go –

Ellie walked on in the glorious Autumn sunshine, aware of the colours, aware of the brightness of the day, watching other people enjoying the weather, envying the thickness of their padded coats, their boots, their hats and scarves and gloves. Such things she had once and had no longer but the memory of their warmth, their comfort, their sheer – pleasantness, had stayed with her. It was a day for walking and many were doing just that. No one glanced at her as she passed them, absorbed in their own lives, their own words, their own memories.

Ah, that word. Memories. They came with the ability to cut, to hurt, to heal, to please, to fill the heart with joy. There were few of the latter and many of the former. Why was life like that, why was it so hard to find the good in life and so easy to remember the bad? Surely the golden days should stand out, days like today, when the weather was perfect and the carpet freshly laid for all to see and admire?

Everything has to end. Everything has an end. Ellie had reached the end.

She walked and the Autumn leaves were not disturbed by her passing over them.

I've Been Waiting So Long For You
(A medieval love story)

Antony walked toward me, tall, handsome, assured, clad in black doublet embroidered with gold, the sleeves slashed with matching colour fabric. I glanced down at my own black gown, lightened with a touch of cream and felt a quiver at the thought we had worn the same colour, we who had never met before.

He took my hands in his; I felt the strength of his emotions more than his physical body. 'Elizabeth, I've been waiting so long for you.' He spoke soft and low and, even as I wondered at his words, I knew the rightness of them.

"Why say you these words?" I blushed and wondered why I had asked such a thing when I had only just met this man – this love. For I knew it in that instant.

"I know not. Only that they seemed right." He smiled and I was completely lost.

This was the man our mothers desired me to marry; both his and mine. They sat huddled on a stone bench for the day was cold; the rooms in the castle were unheated, no order had come for fires to be lit. They watched us as we walked toward one another; observing what we did, listening to what we said. I saw their faces light up, they visualised a money match where I wanted love. I knew, in the words he uttered, I had found that love.

I felt no chill from the ancient stone walls. Instead I looked into the dark brown eyes of my new love and thanked God that my previous husband had suffered an apoplectic fit. That death seemed an age in the past. I recall being relieved that the burden had been taken from me. There had been no love between us.

The man I loved was standing before me.

I had been waiting a long time for him, too.

Halcyon days after the simple wedding ceremony. Halcyon days of being loved. From the first night we slept as one, curved against one another as if we had been married nigh on fifty years and knew the other's body well. We completed each other's sentences and complemented each other's thoughts.

And yet I walked with fear as a constant companion, a shadow I could not rid myself of, no matter the torches lit or the fire which blazed. It walked alongside me.

Court was a dangerous place to be. The enmity, the lingering dissents of the York/Lancastrian conflicts, ran deep and the small cuts it made; the one upon the other, still had opportunities to cause blood to flow. My beloved had fought at Towton, had survived that carnage. Would it ever be so? I knew well that at any time arrays could go out, battle would be waged, men would be killed.

But I had to dismiss these thoughts, I had to live each day for all that it would give us, my beloved and I. And so we rejoiced in our love and our homes and our lives.

I remember well the day he came home bursting with importance.

'I have news but swear on your life that you will tell no one until it is announced!' Never had I see my husband so excited and apprehensive, the conflicting emotions were written clear in his expression, which in itself was unusual. In court one learned to keep all emotions under tight control, for fear of giving offence to the wrong person. It was easier to be dismissed from the place of power than to gain entrance to it.

'I swear," I said, with a touch of fear. I had no idea of how dramatic the news would be but felt it could not be entirely good.

'My sister is married to the king.'

I was silent for what felt like half the day but was surely no more than a few moments. I watched Antony, the ever-changing expressions: delight, apprehension, joy, worry, alternating across the face I knew so well and loved so much.

'Everything changes,' I said at last. It seemed a feeble response but in truth, Antony took it for what it was, a verdict on the happening.

'You have gone to the very heart of it, Elizabeth. Everything changes. Imagine what the court will make of this when the news is given! A Lancastrian widow with children married to the Yorkist king! God's truth, it will cause uproar!'

'Your mother...' I began, recalling the proud determined matriarch.

'Mother is finding it hard to be silent but Edward has so ordered it until he gives out the news himself. I know not what his motive is, unless Elizabeth be with child and he wishes none to know of it.'

108

He paced, snatching up a drinking cup, sipping the ale, putting it down again, seemingly not knowing how to contain his energy, his emotions. I found no happiness in the news, in truth I found nothing but dire warnings of a difficult future. It had been good, living our lives, attending court just enough to ensure His Grace knew we were there but not so much that he would demand too much of Antony. Now it would be different, now he would be related to the king. There would be more duties, more demands and a good deal of animosity. I knew well the Woodvilles were not that welcome in court and to think all of them, the other eleven Woodville siblings, would be there seeking marriages and positions... I could almost feel the poisoned looks and hear the caustic words before they happened.

'It will not be good,' Antony whispered almost to himself; then came over to enfold me in his arms, the one place I felt safe. 'It will not be good for all of us but, my beloved wife, if we handle this carefully, it could be good for us. I am already on fairly good terms with Edward; it will not take much to ensure we have a better relationship.'

'Edward is one thing,' I told him, 'it's his brothers who are of concern to me. I trust them not.'

He smiled. 'This I know, this I am aware of, love of my heart. Be sure I will watch them both with great care.'

I confess our lives were enriched by the marriage. Antony was Cupbearer at his sister's Coronation, he was made Treasurer with all the additional riches that gave us; he took part in an elaborate tournament with Antony, Count De La Roche, to great acclaim. He was made Lord of the Isle of Wight and we travelled there often to stay at the castle. It was good. We were feted and welcomed everywhere we went as if we were royal ourselves. The new queen played her part to perfection, observing every ritual, missing nothing that would endear her to the courtiers and nobles, who were still suspicious of the Woodvilles. I wondered if that was what she carried as her darkness. She produced her children diligently, one a year, Edward produced his bastards, at least one a year that everyone knew of but none spoke about.

And none knew, or if they did they spoke not of it, that Clarence was conniving with Warwick to take the throne from his brother. Much as my beloved husband kept watch on the Yorks for his own safety and mine, he did not know of this until it was too late to attempt to stop it.

The vagaries of Fate! Antony became entrapped in Norwich, held prisoner by Warwick's men, whilst his father and brother John fought at Edgecote against Warwick – and were executed after the battle. When he regained his freedom, my beloved realised he had inherited a new title at the greatest cost of all, the loss of his father. Night after night I held him as he cried out his grief. He had adored and respected his father, to have him die at the hands of Warwick was not something he could easily accept. And John, shining star of the Woodvilles, knight, soldier, brave and upright man, also dead at Warwick's hands. These were losses Antony could not countenance for a very long time.

I watched him lose weight, saw the darkness shadow his eyes and knew that, like me, he carried forebodings. Nothing in life was certain, no matter how many titles you carried, no matter the honours heaped upon you; honours were given for reasons and that reason was often one that best suited the giver, His Grace Edward IV, more than the receiver.

Were we not right to worry? Warwick on the move, Edward indolent and allowing himself to take his time, ended up fleeing for the coast and exile, just as Warwick had done earlier. Edward took with him his brother of Gloucester and Hastings, among other nobles, and a veritable army of men. Antony went too. I had a hastily scrawled note delivered by messenger, bringing me his love and his regrets he had to go, but his liege took precedence over a wife. Not in his eyes, I knew that well, but in the eyes of the king who had left his wife and brood of children in his haste to spare his life.

Bitter? Just a little, methinks.

I confess something now of which only my staff at Sandringham knew.

Each morning he was gone, I would stand in the hall and stare at the door. I would say 'I've been waiting so long for you...' and imagine his smile as I said it.

Each night he was gone I slept alone, longing for the curve of his body against mine, his breath on my neck, his strength comforting and protecting me. Let none speak of the nights I sobbed myself to sleep in the darkness, knowing the darkness did not care, aware of how close Antony had come to dying alongside his brother and father, aware of how

111

precarious his position was in the court, a hated Woodville, an entrusted Woodville, either could turn at any time. I lived in fear, weight falling from me as I supervised our estates, handled our affairs, coped with a myriad of decisions and waited on a messenger with a letter from him, one I could read and read again in the dark hours of longing and emptiness.

I willed him to come home, to come back to me, for without him I was no more than half a person. I managed the estates, managed his finances, consulted with his business manager in London and kept everything going as it should be, but with half a mind and half a heart. The other half was in Burgundy where the royal party had found shelter and succour and were busy with their plans to return. I had letters, travel stained, water stained and soiled from much handling, precious letters which said little and told me so much. I cared not who was sheltering and feeding them, who was funding the ships for the triumphant return, the letters told me that he loved me enough to pay large amounts of money to get them into my hands. The letters were treasured more than all the estates and the gold and the possessions we had.

I heard news of the triumphant return, the storms, the loss of the ship with horses and men, the victorious march down through England. I went to London to greet him, no chance to say the words there, no chance and no need; for we clung together for so long it was all said through our enmeshed hearts. In the embrace London and all who were around us simply vanished into the clouds that still hung over us. Edward was triumphant, yes, but all was not done. It was a long way from peace.

All too soon the array went out to fight Warwick yet again. I had to leave Antony and go home, there were estates to run and business to attend to and, though it broke my heart to go, I had to let the men fight it out at Barnet.

A messenger came to tell me that the king had taken the day, Warwick had been killed and my husband would be returning ere long. That told me he had been hurt, for he would have ridden back with his entourage and brought me the news of the battle himself.

Indeed he was badly wounded, brought back to Sandringham on a litter. All I could think on then was calling the surgeon, the herbs needed, the room in which to nurse him and the fact this time I had my husband back forever and spent my time muttering prayers of gratitude that he was alive, at least. I would not let him go again, no matter what the king said!

'Brave words of a brave wife,' he told me, as I tended the lightning shaped slash of the wound he had in his side.

'Brave actions of a brave husband,' I told him, 'to be in the forefront of the fighting and be wounded in the cause of the Yorkist king.'

'Tis easy enough to forget my Lancastrian background when our lives are at stake,' he whispered through the pain as I changed the dressing, not letting the surgeon go near my man, only to supervise and tell me it would be a long time in the healing. As if I did not know this.

'There will be peace now, love of my heart,' he murmured as he drifted into an uneasy sleep, still clutching my hand.

And for a long time it was so.

Life is never smooth, never without boulders, it was as if we walked on stones and only occasionally did our feet find the places where the earth was soft and yielding. There were problems, there were bereavements, Antony's mother dying was both a sadness and a relief, for she had only existed since her husband had been executed. I knew the feeling so very well. I cried no tears for the proud lady who loved so hard and fought so much for her family. She had gone to rest, which she had long since deserved.

And my rest was coming.

I knew of the treacherous lump and that which it indicated had invaded my body. I said nothing to Antony, afraid of his reaction, praying it would go away. I said nothing when he went serve in Brittany though it meant another separation. I said nothing when his fingers found the lump when he returned that dull November and he went stiff and silent as he explored it. I said nothing when I turned and found his face wet with tears, as mine was.

It was hard that Christmastide, keeping the Twelve Days at court, pretending to enjoy ourselves, taking part in the revels, not wanting to reveal anything to others, but knowing every day was taking its toll. The disease spread fast, I could not fight it.

114

Spring came with a promise of lushness, bright flowers and emptiness. The room in which we slept became my resting place, my sanctuary, for a while. Then Antony, in fear of hurting me by moving in his sleep, arranged another room for me, one I had long favoured. He had it prepared and then he carried me there. I had to hold back my tears for the feelings it gave me, his arms, his strength, his love.

The room was bright and cheerful. Day by day fresh flowers were brought from our gardens; all sign of sickness was banned, hidden away. He had a chair beside the bed and spent all his time with me. Eleven years we had, eleven years of riches and conflict, of business and of social life at court. We had no child, we had one another.

So short a time, so long in the memories it had made. If it were not for the disease determined to conquer me, anyone would have thought I laid abed because I chose to, not because I had to.

Spring dissolved into summer, I grew weaker and I now understand, delirious at times. Antony never, for a moment, let me know I was a burden to him.

In September, after receiving the Last Rites, I slipped quietly from my skeletal body and stood behind my husband, trying to console him as he cried onto my paper thin skin and tired bones.

Time does not stand still. No one can live in intense grief forever; it would be the end of their sanity. My beloved began travelling, making pilgrimages; he began writing, translating works into English, studious works, edifying books. He

115

knew not that I put these opportunities before him and urged him to take them. When he held his first book, his sense of pride was overwhelming and for a moment I saw him look for me, in memory of the many times we shared such momentous occasions. Then he turned back to Mr. Caxton, they shook hands and were pleased with what they had done.

He was appointed tutor to the young Prince of Wales, leaving our home to live at Ludlow Castle with the boys. They adored their Uncle Rivers and went to him for everything. They were the children we never had, he loved them in return.

And I was ever close to him, for I feared for his future.

He married again, after eight long empty years, but I doubt the poor lady had much in the way of his love. Affection, yes. Love, no. She had not been privy to the lonely years as I had.

The messenger who brought the news of the death of Edward IV to Ludlow brought the beginning of the end for my beloved. I knew it, he did not – at the time but I believe he knew something was amiss. But still, he prepared for the journey to London with the new young king as he did with everything, thoroughly. A great army of armed men surrounded Edward V, his brother and my husband, enough to intimidate and impress the people in the towns and villages they passed through, not enough to intimidate and defend him from Richard of Gloucester who had Antony arrested for treason and confined to Sheriff Hutton castle – in truth, a prison.

And now my time drew near. For so long I had walked with Antony, tried to guide his pathway, tried to advise but now there was nothing left to do but sit with him as he waited out the time before his execution. No one said it would happen, everyone knew it would. One of the queen's shadows came back to haunt her, a pre-contract made her marriage to Edward invalid, the boys bastards, her son unable to inherit the throne.

For the Woodvilles, the writing was clearly on the prison walls. All this Antony heard and mulled over during his fifty seven days of solitude and imprisonment, fifty seven days of knowing his life was to end. I stood by as he wrote his will, sent instructions to his business manager, sent messages to his new wife and spoke aloud to me, as if he knew I was there.

In the long, lonely hours he talked of the life we had, the way we were together, the laughter, the tears, the work and the play. I knew then that nothing we had shared had been lost, from the most casual walk in the gardens of Sandringham to journeys to Caister, Middleton and other homes he had and enjoyed. He spoke of Carisbrooke and the great towers he had commissioned and would not live to see. He spoke of my last days and how they tore at his heart and soul.

I knew not then whether he knew of my presence or whether he spoke out of the loneliness and the great love that we had. It mattered not. I heard and I was comforted.

From Sheriff Hutton to Pontefract Castle, to an appointment with an axe. His nephew Richard Grey

117

and his friend Thomas Vaughan were also due to die. Richard was just 19 but I told myself my beloved had fought at Towton a year younger than that. Males grow up fast when there are battles to be fought.

The morning of the 25th June 1483 dawned clear and bright, with birdsong and colour. Antony had written a ballad the night before; I watched the words appear on the vellum, noted the line 'willing to die' and knew it to be true.

I stood waiting outside the castle, as I had stood so many times at Sandringham, waiting, waiting. This time it would be rewarding, this time we would be reunited forever. I had the words on my lips; I held them as if they were captive butterflies.

He came wearing black as he did that first time. He came solemn, as the moment required. He came proud and strong and determined, knelt down without a word to Ratcliffe, who was supervising the executions for Gloucester. Knelt down and let the axe fall and sever his head from his body.

And his spirit stood proud and tall and walked toward me with a radiant smile.

This time it was I who said, 'I have been waiting so long for you.'

THE END OF "VARIETY"

www.ingramcontent.com/pod-product-compliance
Lightning Source LLC
Chambersburg PA
CBHW011516170626
46810CB00009B/3394